James Barclay's

D1322520

Scottish CHRISTMAS CRACKERS

LANG SYNE PUBLISHERS LTD.
GLASGOW

Published in 1996 by Lang Syne Publishers Ltd.
Clydeway Centre, 45 Finnieston Street, Glasgow G3 8JU
Printed by Dave Barr Print, Glasgow.
Origination by Newtext Composition Ltd. Glasgow.
Cover Design by Andy Paterson at New Design Scotland.
ISBN 185217 033 6

Contents

Introduction

Sit back, relax and enjoy a smashing collection of Scottish stories for Christmas by James Barclay, bestselling author of *Paras Over the Barras* and *The Bigot*. His original tales capture the spirit of the season, featuring Jesus, miracles, angels and Santa Claus.

Meet Joey, the wee boy who has never seen a Christmas tree; the bank robber kept on the straight and narrow by divine intervention; the little old lady whose dearest wish is to win the church Christmas cake competition; the three wise Scots men who came from nowhere; the man whose prayers were answered in the most unexpected way; angels who gave Tom Brown wings; Ralph and his incredible dog; Felix, the islander who cannot live down setting his church alight; the loneliest Santa of them all; Alex, master of the universe; the lesson of Maggie's woollen scarf; and Mr Tramp, walking tall in his new boots.

Full of James Barclay's trademarks – human warmth and biting wit – these tales will cheer the heart on cold midwinter days.

Ralph

The Christmas Eve service was over and the church had emptied. Only Old Bob remained sitting there, near the back and convenient to the door. Bob had no need to hurry home. There was nothing, and nobody, waiting for him. He had gone into the church for its warmth...but had enjoyed the service for all that!

The young minister had talked about Christmas and what it all meant...It meant nothing to Bob. Christmas was for other people...for families. Bob had seen his cronies down at the Old Folks' Home die off one-by-one and, if this young minister was correct, THEY were all better off than he was.

He smiled at the thought of Charlie and Benny and grumpy old Hector whooping it up in some heavenly lounge bar. He envied them, not for the celestial nectar they were enjoying, but for the companionship they were enjoying! Loneliness was the great curse! Bob's son and daughter were somewhere in the other side of the world. He hadn't heard from them in years and this saddened him. For hadn't his lovely Annie brought them up 'proper'? Annie, too, was gone now – probably up there looking after Charlie, Benny and Hector! For Dear Annie was *always* looking after folk. It was in her nature. Bob smiled, yes, Annie would be fussing around and arranging the Christmas feast...although, up there, it would probably be a Birthday feast.

Bob was brought back from his thoughts by the sound of a discreet cough. He looked up. The young minister smiled:

"I don't think we've seen you here before!" he said. Bob shook his head:

"Naw, Ah'm no' really wan for church," he replied, quickly adding, "if ye don't mind me sayin' so?"

The minister smiled:

"You're here tonight!"

"Aye, well...er...it was a place tae go," Bob said, feeling slightly embarrassed.

"Have you no family?"

"Oh, aye," Bob said quickly, "ma son and daughter...but they're abroad right noo."

The minister nodded. He understood.

"How did you like the sermon?" the minister asked.

"Fine...jist fine," Bob said, "but...er...Ah personally don't go in a lot for whit ye were on aboot." He hoped he hadn't hurt the young man's feelings.

"Oh, and what didn't you agree with," the minister asked, knitting his brows.

"Well, a' this aboot Guardian Angels an' that." Bob felt a bit more at ease now. The minister smiled.

"Oh, I can assure you that we all have one," he said.

Bob shrugged:

"Whit good is havin' wan if ye canny communicate wi' him. Ah mean, ye'd be as well talkin' tae the wa'...an' Ah dae that anywey." The minister laughed loudly.

"You have a good point here," he chuckled, "but, believe me, he *is* there all the same!"

Bob shrugged. He was not convinced. He stood up and shook the young minister's hand.

"A Merry Christmas tae ye, meenister," he said.

"Robertson," the minister said, "my name's Robertson...John Robertson. And a Merry Christmas to you, too...er...?"

"Jist call me Bob," Bob said, taking the Reverend Robertson's outstretched hand.

He watched as Bob stepped out into the chill of the night, making sure he descended the church steps without a mishap...for the snow had begun to fall again. Bob turned at the foot of the steps and waved.

"And don't forget," the minister called, "he *IS* there."

Bob laughed and gave another cheery wave. Turning his collar up he walked down the street and headed home.

The streets were quiet now. All the last minute shopping was done and all excited children were tucked up in warm beds. Gaily wrapped gifts were already placed under a thousand, winking Christmas trees and exhausted parents were now relaxing.

Old Bob shuffled on towards his one-roomed, his 'Single-End', home. He would brew up a cup of tea, tuck himself up and, in the morning, enjoy the happy cries of the children down in the street. Santa would have done his duty! He wondered if he had any grandchildren? It would have been nice to know – nicer to see them.

It was a clear night now. A full moon shone down and the blue, pulsing stars winked a welcome. Crisp white snow lay thick on the ground and the chill breeze stung at his cheeks.

Bob suddenly stopped in his tracks. He heard 'something'...a whine. He stood listening. All was quiet. He began to walk on but again there was that pathetic whine, a crying! He looked around but could see nothing. He was sure that he had not imagined it. Again he heard it...he looked around and the sad noise was more persistant now. He followed the cry and it led him to a shop doorway.

The shaggy old mongrel lay huddled in a dark corner, shivering with cold and his nose to the ground between outstretch paws.

"Aw, ma wee lamb!" Bob muttered "whit's happened tae ye, eh?"

He bent down and, with some effort, lifted the little, trembling dog into his arms. He opened his coat and tucked it inside...only its face peeking out. He could feel the dog's heart pounding fiercely against his body as he turned and hurried, as fast as his legs would allow, towards home.

His house suddenly felt it was a million miles away but, at last, he arrived at the closemouth. Soon he was inside the house. He switched on the small electric fire. He had not intended to do this. It was cheaper to have his warm, sweet tea and climb into bed. But this wee dog was shaking uncontrollably with a mixture of cold and fear. He rubbed the dog down with an old towel and put it in front of the fire, then, looking through his cupboard, he found the quarter-pound of mince he was saving for his Christmas dinner. He split it in two, putting half on a saucer and placing it before the panting pooch. Bob flopped down on to an easy chair and lit up his pipe. He watched the grateful dog munch into its new found banquet with relish. Finishing the plateful in record time, the wee dog looked up at Bob and then, paws outstretched, lay its head down and closed its eyes. Bob sat looking at the dog for a long time. It was a scruffy looking thing, brown and what was supposed to be white. It wasn't a young dog…but not old either, Bob reckoned. He wondered where it had come from? Had someone thrown him, for a 'him' it was, out? Bob sadly shook his head…there would be a lot like him this seasonal time…after the novelty of having a pet for Christmas had worn off! He sighed, made himself a cup of tea and was soon under the warmth and security of his cosy blankets. In the darkness he could hear the heavy breathing of his new friend. It was a steady, contented deep breathing. Bob smiled, turned over and soon, he too, was breathing in a deep contentment.

A hot tongue licking his face and a cold wet nose exploring his countenance made Bob awake with a start! He sat up quickly. The dog retreated to the bottom of the bed and was lying there, panting with tongue out and, to Bob's mind, had all the indications of a smile on his face.

"Ah, it's yersel'!" Bob said, yawning and scratching his chin. "C'mere, let's have a look at ye." He bent over and pulled the dog towards him.

"Nae collar, eh? An' ye need a bath, that's for sure!" Bob exclaimed. "Ye're just a shaggy wee naebody, just like me, so ye are. Come on, a cuppa tea for me…and a bath for you!"

Bob got out of bed and soon the kettle was boiling on the gas ring. He poured himself out a mugful of steaming-hot tea, sat down in his favourite chair and sipped. He lit his pipe and looked down at the dog, sitting contentedly at his feet.

"Ye're a pretty ugly lookin' dug, aren't ye, eh? Ye remind me a bit like Auld Charlie, God rest his soul, a' hairy-faced. Anywey," Bob raised his mug, "here's wishin' ye a Merry Christmas, wee dug!"

To his surprise, the dog sat up and barked loudly.

"So, ye *dae* have a tongue in yer heid, eh?" Bob chortled.

He finished his tea, tapped out his pipe and pulled out an old basin from underneath the sink, filling it with the remainder of the hot water in the kettle…testing it with his elbow. He remembered Annie doing that with the children.

He got a lather going by rubbing a bar of soap between his hands…liquid detergent was too pricey for Bob's household! Carefully, he lifted the dog into the basin and rubbed the soap in as hard as he could. The dog said nothing and Bob reckoned that he was enjoying the experience. Now scrubbed to the old man's satisfaction Bob gave the dog a good rub down with a towel he had heated at the electric fire, sat back, lit his pipe and was pleased with his morning's work. The dog lay at his feet.

"There ye are, then!" Bob smiled, "Ye look like a completely different dug, so ye dae! Ye're mair like a Wee Benny noo...hairy, but clean!" The dog cocked an ear and raised an eyebrow.

"Aye, ye're a handsome wee dug, right enough!" Bob went on, "but we'll need tae gie ye a name. Canny go aboot callin' ye 'Dug' a' the time...although, mind ye, Ah've met a few blokes called Duggie in ma time. But YOU don't look like a Duggie. Noo, let's see...have ye any preference?"

Getting no reply from this canine waif, Bob stroked his chin thoughtfully. He threw a few names ... 'Rover' ... 'Toby' ... 'Laddie'...across at the dog but got no reaction. "Ah remember, in ma army days," Bob said, "we had a dug at Maryhill Barracks that was the pet o' the lads there...noo, whit was its name again...?" Bob's mind went back and then, snapping his fingers, he cried, "RALPH...that's whit it was called...RALPH, whit aboot that, then, eh?"

The dog jumped up barking loudly, its tail wagging faster than a car's windscreen wiper in a thunderstorm.

"Right, then...that's it," Bob cried, "Ralph it is!" It was Bob's happiest Christmas Day...except for the days when Annie was there and the children crawled all over his knee. Bob left Ralph sleeping soundly and went down to 'the wee shop at the corner' where he purchased a pound of link sausages and a tin of dog food...The feast over, he sat down and chatted to Ralph, who was sitting upright and listening to every word.

"Aye, ye've made me a happy auld man, Ralph," Bob sighed. "Who needs invisible Guardian Angels when they've got a wee dug like you, eh?"

Over the next few days Bob found himself getting more and more attached to the dog. He had acquired a leash and a collar for his new friend and a small feeding bowl. He found himself getting out and about more and found new friends because of Ralph. Children would stop him in the street and give Ralph an affectionate pat. Other folk, out with their dogs, would stop and chat and, down at the Old Folks' Club, Ralph became the pet of the parlour! People saw a great change in Old Bob, too! He was less grumpy and had a smile he never had before. He was more tolerant now...more giving. At night, Bob would settle down in his chair with his last pipe of the day and chat to Ralph about the day's events...now that there *WERE* events to talk about!

The weeks and the months passed and Bob and Ralph were inseparable. Where Bob went, Ralph went. Their nightly chats by the fireside became mandatory...Bob was amazed how quickly the dog learned commands! Ralph could now go down to the corner shop on his own and return with the morning paper. He would dash underneath the bed and come out with Bob's slippers between his teeth the minute the pair returned to the house after a long walk.

Bob had begun to attend the church quite regularly now and Mr Robertson turned a blind eye to Ralph, who would sit quietly at the back of the church until the service was over. In fact, he and the clergyman became firm friends and there was always a treat for the dog afterwards.

It was Christmas Eve...and 'Pension Day' and Bob and Ralph strolled down to the post office as usual on a Thursday. But this was a special pension day. Bob would collect his normal old-age pension...plus the ten pounds Government seasonal hand-out. That would do for an extra treat for himself and Ralph, Bob decided. Bob didn't notice the young man in jeans and denim jacket trail him as he left the post office...not until he entered the closemouth. Bob was suddenly thrown against the wall, pinned by the youth's strong hand around his neck. Bob winced as his head struck against the plaster.

"Right, gie's the money, auld man or ye get this!" A knife flashed and was jabbed against Bob's throat.

"Ye...ye widnae rob an auld man, son, would ye...no' at Christmas?" Bob stammered.

"The money, Pops," the youth said menacingly.

"Take it...take it!" Bob cried, nodding towards his inside pocket...and as he felt cold steel press against his neck. The boy relaxed his grip and fumbled inside Bob's jacket. Suddenly he let out a painful shriek! Ralph's sharp teeth had sunk deeply into his ankles! The wee pooch was suddenly an angry tiger! Ferociously he dug in deeper, his head shaking violently from side-to-side as though he had a struggling prey locked in his jaws. The frightened youth was screaming and trying desperately to kick the dog off. But Ralph's razor-sharp teeth were firmly embedded into his flesh. In the melee, the youth stumbled and crashed to the ground. Ralph was on him in an instant. He pounced on to the terrified boy's chest and, with bared teeth, growled perilously into his face. The trembling youth felt Ralph's hot breath as their noses almost touched. Ralph's growl softened and he sat there...just daring the paralysed youth to make one move.

"Get him aff...get him aff!" the boy screamed. Bob said nothing...He was quite surprised at Ralph's sudden fierceness.

"Please Mister," the youth pleaded.

"Whit did ye want tae go an ' rob an auld man for, son?" Bob said at last.

"A'right, Ralph, let him up," Bob commanded.

Ralph obeyed immediately. The youth rose, staggered to his feet and, with a grimace, rubbed his painful ankle. He kept one eye on Ralph...who was keeping both eyes on *him*.

"Things canny be that bad that ye've tae rob an auld man," Bob said, pushing the youth against the close wall. "Let's see whit ye've got in yer pocket, eh?"

The boy hesitated but said nothing as Bob went through his pockets...Ralph watching closely every move.

Bob had retrieved the boy's wallet and was closely examining the contents.

"You didnae need tae rob anybody, son!" he said.

"It's nearly Christmas," the thief murmured.

"Aye, and that's a time for *GIVING* son, no ' for taking!"

The youth said nothing. He stood, head bowed and with a close eye on Ralph, who hadn't moved an inch.

"Tell ye whit Ah'll dae, son," Bob said, peeling off some pound notes from the contents of the youth"s wallet, "Oor church is havin' a Christmas dinner for the old folks of the parish and are collecting donations. Noo, wi 'a ' this money you've got here, Ah'm sure you would like tae contribute...know whit Ah mean?"

The boy eagerly nodded.

"Oh, aye...oh, aye...definitely," he cried.

"So, whit dae ye say tae me relieven' you o' this five - pound note, eh? That should buy a turkey or somethin'.....and would be maist appreciated."

"Take a tenner, mister, take a tenner!" the boy almost yelled.

"Naw, naw, a fiver will dae," Bob said, "and Ah'll just take this library card, eh? This wan wi' your picture on it...and yer name and address...but you'll no ' be botherin ' any auld soul anywey, will ye, son?"

The youth was silent.

"Right, then!" Bob said with a smile, that's yer good deed for the day. Noo away ye go hame and see the doactor aboot that ankle...and a merry Christmas tae ye, son."

The youth scowled at Ralph and, rubbing his ankle once more, limped out of the close and into the street. Bob looked down at Ralph, now sitting with his tongue hanging out and with what looked, to Bob, a smile on his face.

"My, that's some temper you've got!" he exclaimed. "Who would believe that a wee mutt like you could haun'le a yob like that, eh?" Bob stooped down and gave the wee dog an affectionate pat and was rewarded by a happy wag of the tail. On the way home Bob bought a small Christmas tree... Once inside the house, he placed it on top of the sideboard.

"Ah'm keepin' temptation oot yer wey!" he said, sliding into his chair and lighting up his pipe.

Ralph lay down at his feet and Bob leaned back on his chair. His mind went back to his younger days...those happy days when, at this time of the year, Annie would be busy getting things organised for Christmas Day. The children's presents already bought and gift wrapped and under the tree...visits to Lewis's grotto over. He sighed.

"Ach, Ah'm weary, Ralph, old son, Ah'm just tired. Ah miss Annie and the aulder Ah get, the mair Ah miss her. If anybody was tae ask me what ma greatest wish for Christmas wass, Ah'd say that it was tae see ma Annie again...she'll be young again, noo, eh? Just like she was when Ah first saw her...young and lovely!"

Next day would be the highlight of the year for Bob! The Old Folks' party at the church hall would offer him not only seasonal fayre, but human companionship...even if it was just for a day. He would give the young yobo's money to Mr Robertson and, no doubt, it would be put to good use!

The young minister had told Bob to bring Ralph along, too. As if Bob would have gone without him.

"Aye, we'll have a great time the morra, old boy!" he said, bending down and giving the dog a pat. Bob tapped out his pipe and closed his eyes. Aye, tomorrow would be just fine, he thought! Christmas Day and all the preparations were already made. The long, gaily decorated tables were set out with holly and Christmas crackers in their proper places. In the corner a large fir tree winked with scores of fairylights and streamers and balloons were strategically placed around the room. The minister's young wife and ladies from the guild surveyed the scene with satisfaction.

At twelve noon the hungry, happy pensioners arrived. Mr Robertson and his wife climbed on the dais:

"A very merry Christmas to all of you," he called.

"And tae you!", they choroused.

Soon the steaming hot meals were being served...the turkey and chestnut stuffing, the roast potatoes and all the seasonal trimmings. There was even a dram for the men and a sherry for the women...unless otherwise requested. The hall was soon a hub-bub of happy chatter. The old folk were well into their meal before Mr Robertson noticed the empty seat.

"Where's old Bob?" he said anxiously, turning to his wife.

"I haven't seen him!" she said, a worried expression crossing her face.

"He's not here!" Mr Robertson said, furrowing his brows. "Something must have happened!"

"You had better go round to his house, dear," Mrs Robertson said anxiously.

The young minister wasted no time. There was no reply to frantic knocking at Bob's door...not even a sound from Ralph!

Police were called and a forced entry was made. Bob was still sitting in his favourite chair, his eyes closed and a smile on his face.

"Looks like he's been dead just a couple of hours or so!" the policeman said, straightening up after examining him.

Mr Robertson sighed:

"He was a great old fellow," he said..."Many a good argument we had about the life hereafter...and Guardian Angels. He said he'd rather have his wee dog." The two men laughed.

"Where is his wee dog?" the policeman said, sweeping his eyes around the room.

The two men searched every corner of the house but there was no sign of Ralph.

"That's strange!" the minister said, scratching his head, puzzled. "Ralph's always with him...they're *never* apart!" The policeman stooped down.

"Just a collar here," he said, examining it carefully...

"I just can't understand it!" Mr Robertson said shaking his head.

"Here!" the policeman exclaimed, "Ah thought you said the dog's name was Ralph?"

"And so it is," the minister said nodding.

"Well whit's this name on the collar, then...RAPHAEL? That's no' how you spell Ralph, is it?

Mr Robertson smiled.

"Maybe it was as close to it as Old Bob got," he said.

"Was that no' the name of one o' the...?"

"ARCHANGELS?" Mr Robertson smiled. "Yes, There's Michael, Gabriel...and Raphael...The Three Archangels!"

The policeman removed his hat and scratched his head.

"How about that then, eh! No' only did Old Bob have a Guardian Angel...he had one o' the hierarchy!"

The minister nodded.

"Yes, he had, hadn't he," he said thinking deeply.

"And something else, minister...somethin' that should please you!"

"Oh, and what's that?" Mr Robertson said knitting his brows.

"This Raphael...*HE*...er...wore a Dog Collar, too!

Mr Robertson smiled broadly.

The Christmas Cake

Old Dolly could never afford to enter the church's Christmas Cake competition! It was a case of finances. With her meagre pension it would be impossible to compete with the more affluent members of the congregation. BUT IT WAS HER DEAREST WISH...

Dolly always felt out of place at the services and would sit at the back of the church and "out of the way". Very seldom did she, at the invitation of Mr Kennedy, the young minister, join the company for a cup of tea in the church hall afterwards.

But, more often than not, she would slip quietly away. The ladies who wore the gleaming pearls and fur coats never noticed...although one or two *did* give her a cursory nod now and again.

Dolly felt the years creeping on. And now, once more, the time had come when ovens would be heated and sleeves rolled up. For some reason the old lady thought that this would be her last chance to enter a cake for the contest. Mr Kennedy had announced that the great annual event was now launched and open to all-comers. All cakes had to be at their places in the church hall by seven o'clock on Christmas Eve!

The judge would be, as always, Mrs Penelope Carruthers-Browne...wife of the distinguished Sir Charles Carruthers-Brown, head of the town's super haberdashery store and Justice of the Peace.

Mrs Carruthers-Browne, of the six-bar solid gold charm bracelet, was not noted for her charm. She *did* give generously to the church repairs fund...especially the re-leading of the leaking church roof. It was unkindly suggested that she merely did this to prevent her mink coat getting wet.

Dolly never thought so and gave the noble lady the benefit of her charitable action. The large lady would be fair in her judgement, Dolly was sure of that!

Old Dolly had collected her pension and spent almost every penny on ingredients for her Christmas Cake...her *dream*.

She stood back and surveyed the kitchen table. With a shaking finger, she pointed and began counting her purchases. Yes, everything was there for the cake...even the miniature bottle of brandy. She shuddered at the thought of its price.

Before going to the supermarket Dolly had stopped in at the public library and taken out a book on 'Great Christmas Fayre'...scanning its pages and making sure that she would find a cake recipe that she could afford.

Now all was ready! She had three weeks to bake her masterpiece. This would give her cake plenty of time to mature in its miniature bottle of brandy.

She had bought a tiny Christmas tree, a plastic reindeer and a jolly Santa for the decoration and she smiled happily at the thought of the finished product. The one special ingredient she didn't buy was *love*. But she had plenty of that to put into her beautiful creation!

Dolly worked most of that day, blending and stirring and tasting with her fingertip. Finally, wiping her hands on her apron, she was satisfied.

Solemnly and almost reverently she placed the cake in the oven, checked the temperature with the book and wearily sat down.

Dolly spent most of that day sitting in her favourite chair just staring...at the oven. Now and again she would shuffle up, open the oven door and have a quick peek. She would sniff the baking as it wafted around the room...tempting and tantalizing! Mrs Carruthers-Browne would be surprised that *SHE* had baked such a magnificent cake! Dolly smiled to herself. There aren't many ambitions left to be fulfilled when you are old!

She set the mantleshelf alarm clock for four hours ahead, as instructed. But the hands seemed to go round very slowly as her tired eyes kept constantly glancing over. Very soon she drifted into deep and welcome slumber.

The shrill of the alarm clock awoke her with a start! Had she slept that long? Slowly getting to her feet, she switched the piercing bell off and, with trembling hand, opened the oven door. The heat and the wonderful aroma enveloped her. Dolly turned the gas off and, taking a towel in her excited hands, she tenderly took the cake from the oven. Hobbling over to the oil-clothed table, she laid it down. Removing the grease-proofed paper, she turned it on to a baking board and stood back.

She sat down…and gazed at her wonderful Christmas sculpture. She smiled, satisfied. Her cake was perfect in every way!

Dolly whispered a silent prayer of thanks. She would leave the cake to cool and place it back in the cold oven out of the way in case of accidents.

Dolly had to scrimp for the rest of that week. But she didn't mind. She just had to have a quick peek at her beautiful cake and she was well satisfied.

The following Sunday, after the church service, she could hardly contain herself. Pulling Mr Kennedy aside, her voice shaking with excitement, she blurted out that she had made a cake for the competition.

"Good for you, Dolly!" the young minister beamed and, turning to Mrs Carruthers-Browne, exclaimed: "Hear that? Dolly has made a cake for the competition!"

"How nice!" Mrs Carruthers-Browne murmered and, without a glance at Dolly, turned back to her conversation with her own group.

Mr Kennedy, on the other hand, was delighted and, with his arm around her shoulder, escorted Dolly up the aisle and wished her well.

Soon it was time for Dolly to put the finishing touches to her work of art. With a light touch, she tenderly and lovingly smoothed on the thick marzipan and sweet icing. She would go over it again and again until it was perfect and she was satisfied.

The little fir-tree and the reindeer and the waving Santa Claus was solemnly and ceremoniously placed on top and Dolly stood back and smiled.

It was a work of art! She never thought that she could produce such a beautiful creation. It was a masterpiece!

Tomorrow she would wrap up the cake in a clean dish towel, pack it inside a cardboard box and take it down to the church hall. For tomorrow was Christmas Eve…

Dolly found it hard to sleep that night. She could see the hall, beautifully decorated with multi-coloured streamers and balloons. The Christmas tree would be ablaze with colourful, winking lights. And there, in the middle of the room, would be the long gaily decorated table, covered in seasonal paper and with all the Christmas cakes on top...with flickering pink and white and blue candles with dancing yellow flames waiting to be judged.

Everyone would stand beside their own cake...all hoping to win! Mrs Carruthers-Browne would walk down the line and sample a sliver of each before giving her judgement.

Dolly had often been present at this great ceremony and had always wished that *she* had been standing at the table. And it was a dream that was about to come true.

A few eyebrows would be raised this year at her appearance...and at the wonderful cake she had baked. Who would have thought that 'Old Dolly' could present such a Christmas Cracker of a cake?

Mrs Carruthers-Browne's face would light up with delight after she took her first bite of Dolly's cake. It would be a mixture of shock and surprise. The dignified lady would take another bite...and another and, in sheer joy, throw up her arms at the culinary craftsmanship of this composition.

Dolly floated on in her dream. She had never competed in anything before – never in all her seventy-eight years. Now, in the winter of her life, perhaps HE would present her with a little Christmas gift. She raised her eyes pleadingly. Still, she thought, if HE decided that she should bow out of life – and a good life it had been with Bob – without a rosette, without acclamation, then HE knew what HE was doing. But, it would be nice...just once!

Dolly turned her face to the wall and drifted into sleep...smiling.

She awoke early and the first thing she did was check that all was well with her cake. She put on the kettle and made a cup of sweet tea and got set for the longest day in her life. The clock on the mantleshelf seemed to have stopped and, more than once, she found herself putting her ear to its face, only to hear its steady tick as the seconds passed by.

She viewed the cake again and again, working out permutations for the decorative figures and finally decided to leave them as they were. Before she knew it, the time had passed quickly by and it was the hour to head for the church hall...and, hopefully, her moment of triumph.

Dolly rubbed the condensation off the window pane and stared out into the street. Snow was already falling, a light powder, drifting and covering the street in a soft, white blanket.

A tawny moon shone, glinting in the virgin street. Dolly put on her heavy overcoat and woollen scarf, carefully lifted her prize package and headed down the steep stairs and into the chill of the night.

The sudden coldness took her breath away and she pulled the coat more tightly around herself.

Dolly walked down to the main street, turned right and right again…taking a short cut through the old brickworks.

She saw a group of men, caps pulled down huddled over a crackling fire.

The tramps blew hot air into their freezing hands and almost thrust them into the dancing flames. Dolly felt a lump come to her throat at the scene. Life could be cruel!

She thought about the men as she hurried on down towards the church…saying a silent prayer that some good fortune should come their way this Christmastime!

The church hall was beautiful, just as she expected. Some of the Christmas cakes were already on the table and little groups of women stood around chatting. Nobody noticed that Dolly had arrived…except Mr Kennedy, who approached her with outstretched hand.

"Well, Dolly…a cold night, eh! Come now, let's put your cake on the table," he said with a twinkle. The minister guided her over to the table and carefully took the cake from its box. Holding it at arms length, he sighed with admiration:

"Oh, what a beauty, Dolly! What devotion you've put into this wonderful cake. What a delicacy!"

Dolly blushed with embarrassment. She stammered out a 'thanks' as Mr Kennedy placed the cake down on top of the table saying:

"Now, you go and get your coat off…we'll be starting the judging shortly."

Dolly shuffled into the cloakroom and put her coat and scarf on a peg. Then she quietly entered the hall…finding a seat at the side and away from the gossiping groups.

Mr Kennedy appeared and strode on to the middle of the floor.

Clapping his hands for attention, he said:

"Ladies...ladies...we now come to the big moment. Mrs Carruthers-Browne...do your duty!"

There was polite applause as Mrs Carruthers-Browne approached the table.

"Would all competitors please take up their positions at their own cakes," she commanded.

The ladies hurried to their alloted places and Dolly felt her heart rise to her throat. She took her place and looked around the other entrants, feeling embarrassed to be in their company...and on an equal footing. She sighed! Dolly's big moment had come.

She suddenly felt out of place, like an old mother hen in the presence of young peacocks. They twittered and stood proudly as Mrs Carruthers-Browne took her place at the end of the table and began to slowly walk down the line...like a general inspecting the troops.

Nervously, Dolly wrung her hands as the elegant lady stopped at each cake, cut a sliver and expertly tasted it.

She would then make a comment to its creator before moving on down the line. Dolly saw some jaws drop and others smile. She found her knees shaking as the large, well-groomed lady approached nearer and nearer.

Suddenly she was there...beside her. Dolly could smell the expensive perfume of this lady who elegantly picked up the knife in her well-manicured hand. The hall lights caught her clear nail varnish, making her long, tapered fingers flash like a cluster of diamonds. Delicately, she cut a slice from Dolly's cake.

Dolly was afraid to look. She did not see the grimace on Mrs Carruthers-Browne's face and it seemed an eternity before the lady spoke. Dolly kept her eyes tightly shut and her fingers crossed.

"OH, MY!" Mrs Carruthers-Browne muttered." This cake is tasteless...it has no body...no richness...very bland! A christmas cake should be RICH...RICH!"

Dolly's heart sank. She felt a tear ooze out from the corner of her eye...a drop she quickly wiped away with her sleeve.

The award was given to a well-dressed lady down the line and there was polite applause as the lucky winner chirped her thanks.

The ladies then gathered together and fell into their own little prattling groups.

Dolly stood alone, looking down at her pride. She couldn't believe that her great dream could be shattered and discarded so quickly! Mrs Carruthers-Browne was busy chatting to friends. Dolly did not exist. There was to be no commiserations, no squeeze on the arm with a 'well done'.

It was Mr Kennedy who hurried over to Dolly's side and tried to cool the sting. Putting his arm around her shoulder, he gave her an affectionate squeeze.

"Don't worry, Dolly," he said, "there's always next year!"

Dolly smiled her thanks. Next year? Would there be a next year?

She shuffled into the cloak room and collected her coat and scarf. She wrapped up the cake in the dish towel and slowly placed it in the cardboard box. She turned at the door. Conversation and laughter filled the hall. Dolly sighed and stepped out into the freezing night. Snow continued to fall as she turned towards the brickworks, making her way home.

The Down-and-Outs were still huddled over their dying fire. They looked up as Dolly approached.

"Spare a copper, missus?" one of the shivering men called, holding out a grubby hand…

Dolly shrugged: "Sorry, son," she said softly, "Ah hivnae got tuppence masel' but here, get intae that."

Dolly handed the cake over. The man with the outstretched hand jumped to his feet and eagerly grabbed the box, his eyes beaming with gratitude.

His mates gathered round with hungry eyes as he unfolded the tea towel. Their eyes widened when they saw the glistening Christmas cake.

The man quickly divided the cake evenly and passed it around the group. Hungrily, the men filled their mouths, wiping dirty hands across their lips and savouring this heaven sent, unexpected gift.

"God bless ye, missus," the first man said, taking off his cap. A thankful statement echoed by a chorus of well-filled mouths.

Dolly smiled:

"It's ma pleasure, son," she said quietly and with true meaning.

The men gathered around her and some even tenderly kissed her cheek.

"Know somethin', missus?" a little man with a frayed skipped cap, said between mouthfuls. "Tae get a crust offered tae us would have made oor day. But THIS!"

"Aye," said another, "it's a banquet fit for a king!"

"Well, it *IS* a king's birthday, isn't it?", Dolly smiled.

"Aye, ye're right there, missus," the first man agreed. "And this is the only Christmas present we're likely tae get! But *WHIT* a gift!!!"

"Youse like ma cake, then?", Dolly asked hopefully.

"LIKE IT? LIKE IT?" the men chorused.

"Ah'll tell ye this, missus," the wee man with the frayed cap said, still chewing, "This is the RICHEST Christmas cake that has ever been made, so it is. You've put a loat o' work intae that cake, missus. It is definitely the finest and richest cake Ah've ever tasted!"

Dolly held back the tear. She was suddenly proud. She looked at the unfortunate men tucking into her cake with relish and appreciation.

The snow was now falling heavily. Dolly looked up at the heavens. What *IS* acclamation, she wondered? She suddenly felt that she had won the greater prize!

Her thoughts were disturbed by the happy chorus of the men singing 'Silent Night' as they, once more, huddled around the fire. The cardboard box, too, had come in handy.

"A Merry Christmas tae ye a'," she said, clearing her throat.

"And tae you, tae, missus," the men echoed in unison. "And many o' them, hen. Ye're a wee angel, so ye are, a wee God's messenger," the wee man with the frayed bunnet's voice cried.

Dolly smiled a little embarrassed. She flicked a snowflake from the tip of her nose and pulled the woollen scarf tighter around her neck...and walked proudly home!

Joey's Star

Joey was different...and the boys in the children's ward at Rosevale Hospital didn't let him forget it... When he hobbled past their beds they would hold their noses and make derisory noises. But the wee boy was used to insults being thrown at him. For Joey was a 'tinker'.

He was one of the 'Travelling People', son of a gypsy and grandson of a gypsy. In their battered old caravan, Joey and his mother would travel all over the country...never allowed to put down roots and often the butt of scorn.

Joey never showed his feelings, how hurtful the cruel jibes were. He saw no hope in this world for himself or his weary mother.

They had arrived at the small town just days ago when catastrophe hit them. It was Joey's duty to look after old Francie, their true and faithful old horse. It was while grooming Francie that a wasp stung her and, frightened, she reared and accidentally kicked Joey...breaking his leg.

The ambulancemen were very kind as they rushed him to the hospital. But Sister McKenzie immediately showed her feelings as he was wheeled into the ward.

"Into the bath with him", she snapped.

Now, his operation over and his leg encased in plaster, Joey was "up and about".

It was while sitting in the big chair at his bedside that Joey's eyes widened in wonderment. He watched almost mesmerised as two burly porters carried in the big tree and stood it in a pot at the end of the ward.

"What's that?" he asked, turning to Willie Thomson, who was lying on top of the next bed to Joey. Willie was the only boy who had shown him any kindness and they had become firm friends.

"That's a Christmas tree," Willie said, with just a slight note of scorn. "Don't you know what a Christmas tree is?"

Joey shrugged. He'd never been so close to a Christmas tree

before. When you're on the road there's no place for Christmas trees...or Christmas for that matter. Besides, Joey had contemptuously placed Santa Claus into the land of mythology from a very young age.

Willie was very excited.

"Tomorrow we'll decorate the tree," he said with enthusiasm. "Sister McKenzie told me."

"It's all rubbish!" Joey said. "The whole story...the stable, Santa Claus...all baloney!"

Willie sat bolt upright.

"It is not!" he snapped, "Santa comes when you're asleep and leaves you presents. He's been coming to MY house for years."

"He's never been to mine," Joey said softly.

"That's because you're never in the one place. If you move about all the time, like you do, how is he supposed to know where to find you?" Willie had a little sadness in his voice.

Joey didn't answer. But nothing would change his mind. Christmas and Santa Claus were just bunk.

But Joey found it hard to sleep that night. He felt childish excitement run through his body. He had never been up close to a Christmas tree...never mind help to decorate one.

Right after Breakfast and the doctor's rounds Sister McKenzie stormed into the ward.

"Right, children," she snapped, clapping her hands together, "let's be having you. Only two more days to Christmas and this tree will have to be decorated."

There were screams of delight as the children hurried to the large table in the centre of the ward and sat down.

Sister McKenzie clapped her hands together once more and signalled the porter to bring in the large cardboard boxful of decorations...which had been carefully packed away after last Christmas's celebrations.

The children shuffled excitedly in the seats.

"Right, now children I'm going to give each of you a task." Joey was shuffling harder than the rest!

"Now, you, Willie," Sister McKenzie said, "YOU check that all the little fairy lights are screwed in properly. And you, Mary-Ann, see that none of the baubles has been broken. Each child received a task. But Sister McKenzie had hardly looked in Joey's direction.

"Right, off you go now," Sister McKenzie said, "we want the tree to look pretty while we're all enjoying our turkey and jelly and Christmas pudding, eh?"

"Yes, Sister," went the chorus.

"You haven't given me anything to do," Joey said tugging at Sister McKenzie's dress."

"Haven't I?" she said, looking down into his wide, dark eyes.

Joey shook his head.

"Right, then," the Sister said, "you take that silver paper and make a big star to sit on top of the tree."

Joey almost danced with joy. He immediately threw himself into his task. Firstly he cut out a large star shape from a piece of stiff cardboard and spent the next hour meticulously attaching the silver paper until it was, in HIS eyes, perfect. He held it at arms length and admired his handy work...done with loving care and dedication.

"For a wee bloke who doesn't believe in all this, you've put a lot into that star, Joey...and it's beautiful!" Willie Thomson slapped Joey on the back and the wee boy's chest puffed out three inches. He couldn't wait to present it to Sister McKenzie who took it from him, held it out and studied it carefully...and grimaced.

"It's dreadful!" she snapped, "I could never allow such a tatty star to sit atop OUR tree!" And, with that, she contemptuously threw it on to the floor.

Joey bent down and took it up.

"It's a load of tripe anyway!" he muttered.

Still, there was the Christmas dinner to look forward to. He'd never tasted turkey before...OR Christmas Pud for that matter...and Willie Thomson had said that Santa would come and bring a present. Joey didn't believe that...but there was always the food. Joey fell asleep still clutching his silver star.

Next morning, after the doctor's rounds, Sister McKenzie stood at the foot of Joey's bed.

"Right!" she snapped, "up you get. You're going home today."

Joey felt his heart drop.

"Bu..but tthat means I'll miss Christmas dinner," he stammered holding back a tear.

"Can't be helped," the Sister said, turning down the bedclothes. One of the young nurses passing saw the look of dismay on

Joey's face and her heart went out to him.

"Can't you let the wee boy stay in for just one more day?" she pleaded. "He hasn't much to go home to."

Sister McKenzie shook her head.

"Rules are rules," she said coldly.

"I've seen them bent before," the young nurse said, her face flushing with anger.

"He's going home, back to his caravan...and that's final!" Sister McKenzie was adamant.

"You can take your silver star with you," she sneered.

Joey lay in his caravan bed that night and could see the bright moonlit sky through a gap in the roof. He wondered if Willie Thomson was right but quickly shook his head.

"What nonsense!" he muttered.

Willie Thomson and the rest of them could live with their fairytale, he decided. HE was a man of the world...a man of the road...a TRAVELLER!

Joey listened to bells from the town church. Christmas Eve had arrived. He heard the singing of the choir...'Oh Come All Ye Faithful' echo across the valley. Joey fell asleep, still clutching his star. There had been no flying reindeer streaking across the night sky.

"Joey...Joey..." The voice was soft and low. Joey awoke with a start. The big man with a long, white beard was leaning over him. The man put his finger to his lips.

"Shh," he said, "come on...follow me."

Joey rubbed his eyes and sat bolt upright. His mum was sound asleep in the other bed.

Quietly, he slipped on to the floor, put on his sandals and stepped out into the cool night air.

The big man with the white beard and red attire was waiting for him...beside a large, heavily laden sleigh and with a team of reindeer with shining coats.

"Yo..Yo...You ARE Santa Claus, aren't you?" the boy stammered.

"Ho-Ho-Ho," the big man chortled, "Of course I am," he chuckled. "Come on...climb aboard..."

Joey shook with excitement. He held up his silver star.

"Give it to Rudolph," Santa Claus said, nodding towards the

leading reindeer. Joey laughed and attached the star to Rudolph's antlers and, with a strong hand from Santa, he was swept up on to the sleigh.

"GO!" Santa cried with a snap of the reins. And off they went...right up into the sky. Joey sat mesmerised.

"Where are we going?" he asked, bewildered.

"We're going back in time, Joey," Santa said as they silently zoomed across the sky. "We're going to a place called Bethlehem," Santa added.

Soon Joey could see the desert sand 'way, 'way down below. He did not see the three men on camels gazing up and following his star which had caught the moon's light and shone and glittered and twinkled.

With one mighty tug of the reins, the deer came to a sudden stop.

"Right, down you go," Santa Claus said, "See, down there...that stable...away down and have a look."

Joey almost floated to the ground. The light from oil lamps flooded out of the stable. Quietly, Joey peered in.

A woman was there beside a crib where a little baby cooed and gurgled. There was a man there, too...the baby's father, Joey decided.

Some oxen were moving slowly around, chewing at the straw.

"Excuse me...excuse me...please." Joey turned and stood aside to allow the three men who had been following his silver star to enter.

He watched, bewildered, as they fell to their knees in front of this little boy. Then Joey suddenly realised what was happening. He smiled as he turned and clambered aboard the sleigh once more.

"GO!" Santa snapped and off they went...soaring into the moonlit sky.

Joey sat up with a start. He was in his own bed and his mother was sleeping soundly nearby. He wondered if it had all been a dream until he noticed his silver star was missing.

A note, pinned to his pillow, said.

"Thank you for the star, Joey. Rudolph has gotten quite attached to it and you'll see it every Christmas Eve winking down at you, Santa."

Two days later, on Boxing Day, Joey had a visitor. Willie Thomson, now discharged from hospital, arrived with his new, super mountain bike.

"See," he said, "Santa DID come and brought me my bike. Did he bring YOU anything?"

Joey smiled a thoughtful smile.

"Yes," he said, "he did."

"Well, what did he bring you?" Willie said.

"HOPE!" Joey said.

A Pair of Boots

It was Christmas Eve and the snow had stopped falling, leaving a black satin sky clustered with sparkling, blue stars. The large yellow moon hung like a lantern, bathing the city centre streets in a soft light.

The old tramp turned into the main shopping street, his frozen feet squelching on three-inches of snow carpeting the sidewalk. Christmas trees flashed from shop windows...the bright colours reflecting on the chrystalised roadway. At the top of the street the old church stood out like a Christmas cake in the floodlights.

The wet snow had seeped through the cardboard lining of the old tramp's tattered shoes, numbing his weary feet. He cleared the layer of snow from one of the pedestrian benches, and with a deep sigh, sat down. People were hurrying to-and-fro going about their seasonal business. Happy folk, wrapped in soft woollen scarves and warm top coats! Some wore fur ear-muffs and heavy gloves and, nearly all, carried bright plastic, well-filled shopping bags, emblazoned with fir trees and jolly Santas and packages tied with coloured ribbons.

The tramp sighed...his eyes going to the cobbler's shop facing him.

He stood up and hobbled over to the frosted window and, wiping it with his ragged cuff, peered in. A pair of boots was placed near the front of the window...black and shiny with silver studs. These were a pair of heavy, sturdy boots that any man would be proud to wear, the tramp thought. He sighed and shuffled back to his bench.

A little girl in a red pixie hat had passed by. He watched her tugging at her mother's sleeve and obviously pleading about something. The young mum stopped and began to rummage in her handbag. Taking out a coin, she handed it to her daughter, who gleefully turned about and ran towards the old tramp...thrusting the coin into his shivering hand.

31

"Merry Christmas, Mr Tramp," she yelled innocently and hurried on. The old man stood up, smiled, and, touching his forelock, thanked her.

He didn't notice the young man who had now joined him on the wet bench. The old fellow's watering eyes turned and studied this squatter who sat beside him. He was bearded and in his early thirties and wore a long coat, tied at the waist with a string. A drop-out, the tramp immediately decided. Snow clung to the young man's beard and he looked as down in the heel as the tramp himself.

"Cauld night," the tramp said, making conversation.

"It is that!" the young man agreed.

The ice was broken and the two men sat and talked...and talked. They talked about the state of the world, of politics and religion and this and that and the next thing. As the night wore on the older man began to shiver and the young man noticed:

"Look," he said, "why don't we go up to that church at the top of the street for the Christmas service?" adding, "it'll be a bit warmer, too!"

The old man nodded:

"Great idea, son!" he exclaimed, "But it's been a long time since Ah entered a church. The roof will probably fa' doon!"

The young man laughed.

"Ach, Ah don't think so," he chuckled, helping the old fellow to his feet. The two men set off, walking up the busy street and into the biting wind.

People were hurrying up the church steps, eager to get inside and out of the elements. Some tutted as they passed the pair slowly climbing the stairs...the younger man steadying the other.

A shining, black Rolls Royce glided silently to a stop, it's chrome plating dazzling as it caught the beams of the building's floodlighting.

A small, dapper man, expensively dressed stepped out of the car, checked his gold pocket-watch, grunted and breathlessly climbed the church steps.

The tramp and his new companion followed. The old man noticed that everyone put a donation into a wooden plate at the church door. The man from the Rolls Royce deposited a crisp ten-pound note and strutted inside. The tramp fumbled in his pocket and took out the coin the little girl had given him. Placing it in the collection plate he whispered to his new friend: "That'll dae for baith o' us!" The younger man smiled.

The warmth of the church enveloped them as they stepped inside. The bright lights almost blinded the old man and the organ was already playing softly a carol he knew as a boy. His mind went back to the days when his hard-working mother scrubbed his face with carbolic soap and, firmly grasping his hand, led him and his little sister to the Sunday service. He wondered what had happened to his little sister?

The two men walked down the aisle in the wake of the gentleman with the gold pocket watch. But before they could squeeze into a pew, a firm hand came down on the tramp's shoulder.

"Where dae ye think you're goin', eh?" a gruff voice demanded.

"Ah was just goin' intae..." the tramp began but didn't finish.

The little man from the Rolls Royce forcefully escorted him up the aisle towards the entrance with the younger man following.

"On your way!" he growled. "Look at the state of you...you're filthy! Away an' get a bath!" He turned and said something to the church officer standing nearby and, scowling, once more entered the church.

The church officer was obviously embarrassed witnessing the episode. Apologising to the old man, he said: "I'm sorry old fella but there's nothin' Ah can dae. He's a very important man and donates generously tae the church."

The tramp nodded and said that he understood. The two men walked out of the building and headed down the street the way they had come...and on to their vacant bench. The shops had closed now...the only one remaining open being the shoemaker's shop – it's bright light shining from the window. The two friends sat in silence for a while, each saying nothing but thinking deeply.

"Dae ye think they'll be havin' a party up there?" the tramp said at last, prodding his thumb skywards.

"Eh?" the younger man said, raising his eyebrows.

"Up there," the tramp repeated, "D'ye think they'll be havin' a party...y'know, a birthday party?"

The younger man shook his head.

"I doubt it!" he said. "Not wi' the state the world's in! All those starving folk in the Third World...the intolerance...the greed...people like you with no roof to lie under...cardboard boxes...No, Ah don't see any reason for celebratin'." The young man sadly shook his head.

"Aw, Ah thought the saints might be up there pluckin' turkeys while the angels were pluckin' their harps," the old man chuckled.

Then the light in the cobbler's shop suddenly went out and the shoemaker came out clutching a brown paper parcel. He carefully padlocked his premises, looked up at the night sky, shivered slightly and, turning his overcoat collar up, hurried up the street towards the church. He gave the old tramp a quick glance as he passed by.

The two men watched him vanish in the distance. Snow began to fall again and, from the church, the sound of the carol singers broke the stillness of the night...'Oh, Come All Ye Faithful...Joyful and Triumphant...'

The two men sat quietly, shivering and not talking, but listening to the beautiful sound of a hundred voices. They sat spellbound through the entire service.

It seemed no time at all until they heard distant, hurrying, crunching footsteps approaching from the direction of the church. The shoemaker, breathless and still clutching his paper parcel hurried up to the bench.

"Glad I caught ye!" he exclaimed. "Here...this is for you." He thrust the parcel into the old tramp's hands.

"Fo...For ME?" the old man stuttered in disbelief, fumbling excitedly with the string. His hands trembled with anticipation...and cold and he found the operation of loosening the wrapping very difficult.

"Here, gie it to me," the cobbler said, producing his pipe knife. With one deft slash the string parted. The tramp's eyes widened with a sparkle that hadn't been there for years. The black shiny boots with the silver studs sat nestling in tissue paper. His jaw dropped and he stared at his benefactor.

"Well, go on...see if they fit," the shoemaker said.

"The tramp wasted no time. Off came his battered and sodden old shoes and on went the new, rugged, tough boots that could face any weather.

"They fit like a glove!" the tramp cried with joy.

The cobbler nodded: "Aye, right enough," he said pleased, "it's like Ah made them just for you! Funny, that! Ah really made them for a big-wig at that church. It was tae be a surprise Christmas present frae the church workers. Mind ye, he might never have worn them...maybe no posh enough! Still, THEY said they would be just the thing for him trampin' around his estate. Comes tae church in a big Rolls Royce, y'know. Bags o' money!"

"So, why did ye no' gie him them?" the tramp asked, puzzled.

"They said he had a wee attack durin' the service and was taken tae hospital. They telt me just tae gie the boots away...so there ye are, eh!"

The tramp turned to his friend. "Aw, that's terrible...Ah hope it's no' serious!"

"Ah'm sure he'll be all right!" the younger man said.

"Ah don't know if it's serious or no'," the cobbler shrugged.

The tramp stood up and put his weight on his new boots. "Ah'll have dry feet for the rest o' the winter," he cooed. The cobbler put his arm around the old man's shoulder and steered him away from the bench. "C'mon," he said, "you're comin' hame wi' me tae meet the wife, the weans and the gran'weans...and a Christmas dinner you'll never forget!"

"Aw, that's awfu' kind o' ye, mister...but Ah couldnae leave ma freen'," the tramp said.

"Whit freen'?" the shoemaker asked, knitting his brows.

The tramp turned round to see the young man walking away. Their eyes met. The young man with the beard's were sad...and full of compassion. No word was spoken! The old man found it hard to tear his eyes away from the stranger. The younger man's eyes were full of love and sorrow...and pity.

"Happy birthday, Sir!" the old tramp said, choking slightly.

"And a happy Christmas to you, son!" the man said before turning and vanishing in the now dimly lit street.

"Who were ye talkin' tae?" the shoemaker inquired curiously.

"Aw, just a freen' o' mine," the tramp said, adding, "it's his birthday."

"Oh, aye?...well, come on," the other said. "Let's get hame tae that roastin' fire."

The two men walked into the night. The tramp felt something in his tattered coat pocket. He dug deeply into the recess and pulled out a coin. Funny! He thought he'd given that wee girl's coin away! His new boots crunched down on the new-packed snow and the tramp proudly puffed out his chest…and walked tall!

Charlie's Christmas Present

The two tramps sat on their usual park bench and were glad that the snow had stopped falling. A glistening white blanket covered the small town and an amber moon floated on a black velour sky speckled with blue, winking stars...

Behind them was the main street with busy shops, dazzling with Christmas lights and green fir trees, blinking and flashing with the colours of the rainbow. Happy people, well wrapped up in the chill weather, were scurrying along carrying gaily coloured parcels. All would be heading home to cosy, crackling fires...and to families!

Along the pavement, under the streetlamp, a Salvation Army Band played 'O' Come All Ye Faithful' and was joined by carollers, who paused only to blow some heat into their mittened hands.

Charlie, the elder of the two, wondered if Officer McDonald would come along and move them on...as he was wont to do at times. Although, most often than not, the big burly cop would turn a blind eye...and it wasn't the first time that he 'accidently' let a packet of cigarettes drop in their vicinity.

A shaggy old mongrel wandered up and sniffed around the two men before turning and continuing its nocturnal stroll.

"Wise dug!" Charlie thought. It knew that they had nothing to give. There would be richer pickings in the busy street!

Now and again a police siren could be heard. Shoplifters would be having a busy night. Officer McDonald would be kept on his toes, Charlie reckoned. He turned and looked at his companion. Andy's eyes were closed. Well wrapped up in old newspapers under his tattered coat, he had probably drifted into blessed slumber...and release!

A young courting couple passed by, oblivious to all around them. *EVERY* day was Christmas to them, Charlie thought with a smile. The Salvation Army Band was now playing 'Silent Night' and the young carollers were singing softly. It was one of Charlie's favourites. It was MARY'S favourite. Mary! HIS Mary! He wondered if she had ever forgiven him? He could never forgive himself! The happy laughter of children echoed down the street Happy Families!

All this could have been his! His mind went back more than twenty years. Life was good then! There was Mary, beautiful and loving Mary, who kept their tenement home jealously spotless. Always a hot meal on the table when he got in from work. Always there, fussing and comforting.

Their happiness was complete when baby Jean came along. Jean would be about twenty-four now, Charlie thought. His mind was dimming! Old age and the bottle were taking their toll!

When he lost his job he found the bottle and that became his Loving Cup! It was all in the past now. He had walked out...staggered out...on his little family. The downward slide was easy then. He had heard that Mary had died and that baby Jean had been adopted out. Funny how every Christmas his mind went back to what might have been! As he got older the pain got sharper...like thorns in his side...needling him!

Charlie was never a praying man, although recently he found himself quietly talking to the Almighty begging for forgiveness. It was too late to ask Mary...but maybe HE...if there WAS a 'HE'...? Charlie didn't see why he should be forgiven and he wondered if there was anybody up there listening? Looking at his own ragged, scruffy appearance, he decided he was getting all he deserved. No, there was nobody up there listening! Life is what you make it and he had let his potter's wheel run riot and left his life in a shapeless morass.

Christmas was a nice story invented for children and the gullible!

Charlie had once read that we all have a Guardian Angel...heavenly bodies sent to guide and accompany us through the trials and tribulations of this mortal life. If that were true...where was HIS? How come he had sunk to this gutter level? He must have been allocated the dunce of the bunch, he reckoned.

The wandering mongrel returned and began to bark furiously at the two men on the bench.

"Sorry old son," Charlie said, "ye're barkin' up the wrang Christmas tree here. We've got nothin' for ye!" Andy woke up with a start: "Whit's up?" he stammered.

"It's just a poor wee dug that's in the same boat as oorsel's," Charlie replied with some pity. The dog got the message and ambled off on its foraging safari.

"Aye, just like us," Charlie said into himself. Andy rubbed his eyes and stretched his muscles as Charlie dug deeply into his coat pocket and produced, two, good-sized, cigarette butts that he had retrieved from the door of a pub lounge. He offered one, the largest, to Andy, who declined.

"Ah forgot you don't smoke, Andy," Charlie said, lighting up with a shaking hand and taking a deep drag. Andy blew heat into his own hands.

"This is the only Christmas present that Ah'm likely tae get!" Charlie said, holding up the cigarette.

"Whit would be your ideal Christmas present, Charlie?" Andy asked, flapping his arms around his body to keep the circulation going.

"Oh, Ah know whit it would be," Charlie said softly, a faraway look in his eyes, "Ah know." The two men sat in silence and listened to the band in the street, now playing 'Away In A Manger' and the singers sang with deep and quiet feeling.

The two men sat and listened in silence. Andy was younger than Charlie and was obviously better educated...but never talked of his past. Charlie never intruded. A man's life was his own. All Charlie knew was that he was glad of Andy's companionship. Loneliness was the great disease...Charlie knew that.

"Dae ye believe in prayer Andy?" Charlie found himself asking.

"Definitely!" Andy said.

"Dae ye think there's somebody up there listenin' tae ye...and answers ye?"

Andy nodded, "Ah'm sure of it!"

"Whit aboot Guardian Angels? Dae ye believe in them?" Charlie asked quietly.

"Nae doots!" Andy said.

"Then how is it that we're in the state we're in, eh?" Charlie said sourly. Andy thought deeply.

"Well," he said, "if ye look back on yer life, could it no' be that you got yersel' intae this situation?"

Charlie slowly nodded.

"Aye, ye're right, Andy," Charlie said, adding, "but that only goes tae prove that there's nae Guardian Angel...otherwise he would have...er...guarded me, wouldn't he have, eh?"

"Maybe yer faith wisnae strong enough, Charlie," Andy said.

Charlie said nothing but thought deeply. Then, turning to Andy, he began, on a lighter note:

"D'ye think they've got wings...big wings? Ah mean, if they are heavenly bodies, whit dae they need wings for, eh? If ye ask me, it just makes a nice picture for Christmas cairds...angels wi' wings, a' flyin' aboot." Andy ignored his friend's remarks.

"Angels or no'," he said, "Ah hear YOU prayin' at night when ye think Ah'm sleepin." Charlie shrugged. "Ye've got tae take oot some insurance, Andy," he chortled.

The night got colder as it wore on! The street traffic had begun to quieten down and the chatter and laughter had faded. The Salvation Army Band had already packed away their instruments and moved on and soft snow had begun to fall. Charlie and Andy pulled their coats tighter around their necks. They didn't hear the screech of brakes up on the roadway...or Officer McDonald's crunching footsteps approaching. The big policeman was standing over them before they knew it.

"Right," he said, "taking a firm hold on Charlie's arm and pulling him up from the bench, "you're comin wi' me!"

"Whit have AH done?" Charlie protested trying to free himself from Officer McDonald's vice-like grip. "Ah hivnae done anythin'!"

The policeman ignored his protests and steered him towards the car...the back door lying open. A young, lovely girl stepped out from the car and stood looking at the, still protesting, tramp.

"This is him, miss!" Officer McDonald said, "This is Charlie."

Charlie was still trying to free himself from the policeman's iron grip and, turning looked pleadingly at the girl. "If somebody stole yer purse, Miss, it wisnae me...honest!" he said appealingly. "Ah might be a lot o' things, hen, but Ah'm no' a thief!!" Charlie shuffled his feet. The girl said nothing and Charlie ran a finger under his threadbare collar. He looked at the girl and their eyes met. Tears were welling up in her soft, brown eyes. Charlie's brows furrowed and his jaw dropped open as he looked closer..."Mary!" he found himself saying..."MARY..." but it couldn't be! The young girl began to sob uncontrollably. She threw her arms around Charlie's neck and hugged him tightly.

"Oh Daddy!" she sobbed, "Daddy...Daddy..." Officer McDonald turned away and blew into his handkerchief.

"The young tramp who came to my door was right...it is you! I'm Jean...your daughter...Jean. I've been searching for you for years, Daddy!"

A lump came to Charlie's throat and the tears flooded down his cheeks.

"JEAN? Ma ain wee Jean," Charlie sobbed, "Oh, can ye ever forgive me, ma wee lamb...could ye...?"

Jean hugged him tightly. "Of course I forgive you...and so did mum before she died. SHE knew what you were going through...losing your job...your self-respect...She never had a bad word to say about you, daddy."

Charlie, weeping uncontrollably, rested his head on her shoulder. She comforted him like a baby.

"There, there," she said, "Come on...you're coming home with me. You're coming to YOUR home, daddy, to meet my husband, Tom...and you have a wee grandson, Charles is his name...and he's just dying to meet his grandad!"

Charlie pulled back.

"Ah've got a freen'," he said. "Andy, doon there. Ah canny just go an' leave him!"

"You go and fetch him," Jean said. "He can come and enjoy Christmas with us." She kissed Charlie lightly on the forehead and watched him hurry down the pathway. Andy was standing, waiting.

"It's ma daughter, Jean," Charlie cried, joy in his shaking voice. "She's been lookin' for me for years an' years...for ME! C'mon ma wee pal, you're comin' as well!"

Andy didn't move. Then, shaking his head, he said: "You go, Charlie. It's YOUR Christmas present...the one you've been praying for all those nights when you thought I was sleeping."

The truth suddenly dawned on Charlie. "It...it was you, wisn't it...? You telt Jean tae find me, didn't ye, eh? But how did ye know where tae find her?"

Andy smiled.

"She, too, has been praying, Charlie. And ALL prayers are

heard!" Suddenly his tattered coat fell from him and he stood tall and as radiant as the sun. His golden hair fell over his shoulders and he smiled...a compassionate smile. "Look, Charlie...nae wings!" Andy mimicked and, smiling, he waved a farewell and the light dimmed and Charlie found himself alone. He turned, slowly walked up the pathway and climbed into the back seat of the police car.

"Where's your friend?" Jean asked, knitting her brow.

"Oh...he...er...had a prior engagement," Charlie said quietly. "Ah...er...think he's away tae somebody's birthday party...Ah think." Charlie looked up at the night sky. Jean smiled and thrust her arm through his and held on tightly. Officer McDonald closed the door and climbed into the driver's seat. The siren wailed and they sped off. Jean bent over and kissed Charlie's forehead. He squeezed her hand. He was going home...to his family!

Plane Crazy

Old Tom sipped the last dregs of his tea, pulled back the curtain and gazed into the bleak December morning! He shivered slightly. Just one more week till Christmas! Just another Christmas! The crisp weather hadn't stopped the children from playing in the snow blanketed street. Tom listened to the happy cries of fun and laughter and he smiled to himself.

Tom had never married! He had no-one, no family and, to him, Christmas just meant another ten pounds on his State pension...the only gift he was likely to get! He had never even received a Christmas card.

But Old Tom had his beloved picture collection of aeroplanes. *They* were his family! The walls of his single-apartment tenement home were plastered with them. Tom's family *was* as a gallery of Hurricanes and Heinkels, Messerschmitts and Lancasters and his Piéce de Résistance...the glorious *SPITFIRE*, which was framed in a gold, plastic border above the mantlepiece.

Flying was his life and many a hairy tale of wartime dogfights to the death he recounted to his cronies down at the pub...appropriately named, 'The Flying Duck'.

He met the postman coming up the stairs as he locked his door. The mailman, busy popping Christmas cards through the stair-landing letter boxes, turned:

"Nuthin' for you, Tom!" he said, carrying on up the stairs.

Tom shrugged:

"So, whit's unusual aboot that!" he murmured.

The postman laughed.

"Never mind, Tom," he called, "wan o' these days Ah'll be delivering the *big* wan for you...a cheque frae Littlewood Pools, eh!"

"Ah don't dae the fitba' pools," Tom grumbled, "Ah canny afford it!" He shuffled on down the stairs and into the street. The chilled air stung his craggy face and he pulled up the collar of his old great-coat and adjusted the straps of his tattered leather flying helmet. He had bought the headgear round 'The Barras', in Glasgow's East-End, for fifty-new pence, or, as Tom would say, 'ten-bob'. It was really made for a motor cyclist but to Old Tom Brown it was the insignia of the dashing Spitfire pilot.

He strolled down to the post office, collected his pension and, as usual, headed for the Flying Duck.

His cronies, Sandy and Archie would probably be there, pints of beer in front of them on the table and well into their chinwag!

Sandy glanced up at the old wall clock. Tom would be arriving any second now...he was regular as any regular could be. Sandy nodded over to Jimmy, the barman, who immediately pulled a pint and took it to the old timers' table. Hardly had he placed it down when Tom entered and, nodding to his pals, joined them at the table. He took a long swig at the frothy pint, wiped his mouth with his ragged cuff and leaned back.

"Well, how's it been the day, Biggles?" Sandy said with slight sarcasm.

Tom shrugged.

"Same as usual...same borin' week in fact!"

Archie sighed.

"Aye," he said. "Nuthin' chinges, so it disnae."

There was a long silence as each man sipped his drink. It was Sandy who broke the quiet.

"Ah got a Christmas card frae ma daughter in Canada this moarnin'," he said a little smugly.

"Nice!" Archie said.

"Aye," Sandy went on, "she's gonny have me ower for a holiday when the weather gets better. They've got terrible winters there, y'know...in Toronto!"

Tom looked up.

"How long as she been there?" he asked.

Sandy thought hard.

"Eh, twenty-two years," he replied.

"An' have ye been ower there before...visitin' her, Ah mean?" Tom asked.

Sandy shook his head.

"Naw...it's their winters, y'see!"

"Aye, their winters," Tom murmured and took another sip at

his pint.

"Ah was in Canada wance," Archie piped up. "Durin' the war, it was. Have you ever been there, Tom?"

Tom sat up.

"Och, aye," he beamed. "It was durin' the war, as well. Ah got sent there tae fly some auld American planes ower here via Iceland. Aye, it was bloody caul'a'right." Tom gave a mock shiver.

Archie laughed loudly.

"Ach away wi' ye!" he hollered. "You've never flown an aeroplane in yer life, ye auld coot!"

Tom was hurt.

"How would you know, eh?" he snapped. "There was a lot went on durin' the war that is still in the secret archives…in London…things that, even noo, we are not allowed tae divulge!"

Archie shook his head and chuckled. "Aw, come off it, Biggles, be honest. No' only have ye never *flown* a plane, ye've never been *up* in wan," he said. It's a' in yer mind – it's a high-flyin' dream!"

Sandy nodded.

"We've a' got oor dreams," he said softly. "There's nae herm in havin' dreams."

Tom said nothing. Archie was correct. He had never flown a plane…never even been up in one. But it had always been his dream. As a boy he zoomed across the skies in imaginary adventures. Throttle pulled back, daring loops and a squeeze on the red button that spat cannon fire at the enemy…He *had* served in the Royal Air Force during the war, as a clerk. And it was with slight envy he saw the young pilots scramble to their Spitfires and Hurricanes and scream into the air to take on the Luftwaffe in fearless combat.

And he had waited quietly, watching the sky for the familiar drone that heralded their safe return.

Archie broke into Tom's thoughts.

"Right, it's ma round," he said. "Same again, Jimmy!"

The barman nodded and began pulling the beer.

Archie turned to Tom.

"Noo, tell the truth…you've never flown in yer life…in't that a fact?"

Tom was concerned. He had told so many white lies about his wartime escapades over the years and over that table, that he could not own up now...not to Archie anyway.

"Ah've telt ye before," he snapped, "Ah was known as Ace Broon...wan burst o' ma guns and..."

"Ach, ye're an auld blether!" Archie grunted.

Tom was hurt.

"Is that so?" he cried. "Well...er...it just so happens that Ah got a Christmas card masel' this moarnin'...wi' a very...er...special invitation."

Archie and Sandy's eyebrows shot up in disbelief. They knew that Tom had never received a Christmas card in his life...and positively never an invitation.

"Ah don't believe it!" Archie muttered.

Tom shrugged.

"That's up tae you, believe it if ye like...Ah know whit Ah know!"

Sandy warmed to Tom's news.

"Did ye *really* get a card this moarnin', Tom?" he asked with genuine interest.

"Wi' an invitation," Tom added smugly.

Archie wiped his mouth with his sleeve.

"Let's see it, then?" he demanded.

Sandy leaned over.

"Aye, go on, Tom...let's have a shufti."

Tom shifted uneasily in his chair.

"Well, er...Ah don't have it wi' me," he stammered, "Ah was...er...feart Ah'd lose it...it's...er...a very important invitation y'see."

Archie puckered his eyebrows.

"Whit *is* the invitation, then, eh?" he said suspiciously.

Tom cleared his throat.

"Well, it's...er...an invitation that's only gied oot very seldomly...tae aviators...like masel."

Jimmy arrived with the drinks and each man took a gulp, putting the glasses down in unison.

"Right", Archie said, wiping froth from his chin, "away up tae the hoose and get it. We'll wait."

Tom was startled at Archie's request but Sandy was more practical.

"Don't be daft!" he said. "By the time Biggles shuffles up tae the hoose and gets back doon here again, he'll no be worth a curdy. Nane o' us are young men y'know, Archie." Tom breathed a sigh of relief.

"A'right, then," Archie said, "ye can bring it the morra. Ah can see that ye're no' for tellin' us whit this invitation is a' aboot, anywey!"

Sandy leaned over.

"Is it a secret or somethin'?" he asked, almost in a whisper.

Tom gave a knowing smile but said nothing.

The three old timers finished off their pints. The session at The Flying Duck was over and they got up to go their own ways. In the summer they would go down to the park, sit on their favourite bench and watch the world go by. As they left the pub the snow began to fall. They nodded their farewells and each left for his own corner.

Tom buttoned up his great-coat and shambled along...wearing his leather flying helmet buckled tightly round his ears – and a worried expression!

Tom shuffled along the main street, past the shops and, passing the church, he hesitated. He wasn't a praying man...not that he didn't believe in the Almighty! But, he reckoned, that the Good Lord had more important things to worry about than any trifling hiccups that Tom might have.

Still, no harm in popping in for a visit, he thought. Looking around and making sure that none of his old cronies was about, he climbed the stairs and entered the stillness of the building. His footsteps echoed throughout the rafters as he gingerly walked halfway down the aisle and slid into a pew. He looked around and was glad to see the church empty. He sat quietly, the only sound coming from his own heavy breathing.

His mind went over the events of the morning and he wondered if *HE* would hear, or even *want* to hear, his moans. After all it had been a long time since he conversed with Him. But, he remembered his mother telling him once that anytime he had a problem, he should put his trust in *HIM*. His mother was a wee woman of big faith!

Tom cleared his throat and, in a whisper, began to talk to his invisible listener.

"Ah...er...know Ah hivnae spoke tae ye for a long while," he said with some embarrassment and some guilt…"but Ah was wonderin' if you could see yer wey tae dae me a wee favour?"

Tom stopped and listened. No fork lightning had struck him down and the church roof was still intact. He felt encouraged to continue.

"It's…er…really ma ain fault this predicament Ah've found masel' in. Ye see, Ah've…er…sort of been makin' things up as Ah've went along life's path…nothin' that would hurt anybody, ye understaun'…" he emphasised. "Naw, naw, Ah would never dae that! It's just that Ah, well…er…*invented* things…know whit Ah mean? Daft things…tales aboot ma flyin' prowess durin' the war. See Ah'm just whit Ah am…whit *you* made me. When Ah was a boy, Ah used tae staun and watch the starlings comin' intae the street at night…hunners o' them, soarin' and swoopin'…aw, how Ah envied them!"

He pulled out a handkerchief and gave his nose a good blow as his mind went back to his boyhood days.

"Aw, it was a wonderful sight tae see! An' Ah just wanted tae be just like them…up there in the sky – free as a bird, if ye see whit Ah mean. And, when the war came an' Ah was a young man, Ah wanted tae be a flyer," He paused for a moment and cleared his throat. "But…er…Ah hadnae the education, y'see. A' Ah ever did was push a pen…and watch the other fellas fly. Ah, never, ever got up there…tae the clouds, that is. In fact Ah never really amounted tae anythin'. Never got married…although Ah nearly did wance…but you decided ye wanted ma Jean yersel'. So, there we are, eh! Ah've been tellin' Archie and Sandy a lot o' fibs and they've got me in a coarner noo. They're really a nice couple of auld middens…so it's no' their fault Ah'm in the mess Ah'm in. Ah telt them that Ah' received a Christmas card wi' an invitation…and they've called ma bluff. They want tae see it and Ah, well, Ah hivnae a bloody clue…oops. sorry…who could possible have sent me a card…no' tae mention a bloody…oh, sorry again, invitation."

Tom wondered if *HE* had heard his slip of the tongue. He wondered if *HE* had heard *ANYTHING?* Tom shrugged.

"A' Ah ever wanted tae dae was fly," he said. "Daft, int it. Ah'm sittin' here an' Ah don't even know whit it is that Ah'm askin' ye tae dae for me."

He fell silent and then, getting to his feet, walked up the aisle. He turned at the end of the passageway, blew his nose once more and said:

"Jist forget the whole thing. Forget Ah was here. Ah'm sorry tae have bothered ye. Ye've got that many mair important things tae worry aboot. Ah should'nae have taken up yer time. Anyway, when it comes...'Happy Birthday!'"

Tom turned at the door.

"Roger, over an' out!" he said.

The snow was falling heavily as Tom stepped out into the street. He fastened his helmet, turned up his collar and hurried along as fast as he dared.

He didn't sleep that night! His mind was in a turmoil. How would he face Archie and Sandy when they met down at the Flying Duck in the morning? He considered 'coming clean'...but immediately discarded the notion. Then, again, maybe he *should* tell Archie and Sandy that he was just an old windbag! But, then again, over the years they *did* enjoy his tales of daring-do, he *knew* that. Maybe he had been putting some colour in their lives, taking them out of themselves. Perhaps they were secretly transported back to their boyhood...wide eyed reading The Hotspur and The Wizard. Old men have a habit of going full circle through life! Should he admit that his flying exploits were just pie-in-the-sky?

Tom lay and watched the room get brighter as the dawn came up. He had gone through the night dozing spasmodically. The old wall clock chimed eight and Tom's eyes opened wide. Yes, he *would* tell his old pals that there was no Christmas card...no invitation.

Tom rose, dressed and made a pot of tea. He had four cups before venturing out. Locking his door, he turned and met the postman coming up the stairs with his usual bundle.

"Mornin' Postie," Tom said, touching his forelock.

"Mornin' Tom," the postman smiled.

Tom continued down the stairs.

"Just a minute, Tom", the postman called, "there's somethin' here for you today..." Tom stopped in his tracks.

"Fo...for *me*?" he stammered in surprise.

The postman nodded.

"Aye, a card," he said, pulling one from the pile.

"Ach, there must be some mistake," Tom said, screwing up his lips, "Naebody sends me a card – there is naebody tae send wan!"

The postman checked the address on the card once more and, handing it over to Tom, said:

"Aye, it's definitely for you, a'right...although Ah canny make oot the postmark!" Tom found his hand shaking as he took the card from the postman, who smiled and continued up the stairs, saying, "Ye must have a secret admirer, Tom, eh, ya fly auld midden!" The man laughed loudly as he vanished round the bend in the stairs.

Tom turned and, key shaking, opened the door and went back into the house. He put the card on top of the table and sat down staring at it. The card was in a pale blue envelope and sealed...not like the normal Christmas cards. It could be from the Gas Board, or the Electricity Board or some other faceless organisation wishing him the season's greetings, with a bill enclosed, Tom thought.

He sat gazing at the card on the table for a while before curiosity got the better of him. Hand trembling, he took the card and checked the envelope. Yes, it was addressed to himself all right...even with the correct post code. Slowly, he tore open the envelope and removed the card.

Printed in gold letters it said:

"To Tom, wishing you a very happy Christmas! You are invited to the inauguration flight of Number Five. It will be a real 'Wing-Ding'. We will call for you on Christmas Eve. Cheers, Mike."

Tom scratched his head. He was puzzled. He checked the envelope once more. Yes, it was certainly addressed to himself. Who was Mike, he wondered? An what was Number Five? Possibly this was the reference name for a new plane...as yet un-named. It all sounded too good to be true but Tom was delighted. Now he had something tangible to present to Archie and Sandy down at the Flying Duck. What a surprise *they* were in for...although not as big as one he received himself.

Tom stuffed the card into his pocket and, once more, stepped on to the landing, locked his door and descended the stairs. He stepped into the street with a new spring in his step and rubbed his hands together...not for warmth, but in anticipation of the shock he was about to spring on the two sceptical old middens who would be waiting for him.

Archie and Sandy were, as usual, in their places at the table with Tom's pint ready and waiting for him. Tom entered, sauntered over with his chest puffed out, gave a cursory nod and sat down. He took a swig from his pint, smacked his lips and wiped his mouth. Then he leaned back, a smug expression on his face.

There was silence for a moment until, finally, not being able to contain himself, Archie leaned over.

"Well?" he said showing impatience.

"Well whit?" Tom snapped, being nonchalant.

"Well, let's see it...yer card, yer invitation," Archie said, his eyes narrowing suspiciously.

Sandy nodded.

"Aye, c'mon, Tom, oot wi' it."

Tom patted his mouth with the palm of his hand, pretending a yawn.

"Oh, *THAT*!" he said. "Ah'd forgotten a' aboot that."

Archie gave Sandy a knowing look.

"So, ye hivnae got it, eh?" he said, with a slight sneer.

"Oh, ye want tae see it...is that it?" Tom said.

Tom began to go through his pockets.

"Noo, where did Ah put it...naw, no' in there," he said, prolonging Archie and Sandy's agony.

"Ah, here we are!" he cried in triumph and handed the card over to Archie, whose jaw dropped as Tom thrust it into his hand.

Sandy leaned forward and the two old men read the card, stunned and with some awe.

"Aye, well...er...whose this Mike and whit's this Number Five, eh?" Archie said, handing over the card to Tom, who placed it in his inside pocket.

Tom patted his mouth once more in a mock yawn.

"Well...er...Mike...he's...er...wan o' the top brass, know whit Ah mean?" Tom tapped the side of his nose with his forefinger.

"And Number Five?" Sandy asked with some excitement.

"Well, that's...er...the coded name for a new Fighter Plane wot we are producin'. It's...er...still in the experimental stage."

Tom tapped the side of his nose once more.

Sandy flopped back on his chair, very impressed by this whole episode. Old Tom, cunning devil that he was, had *never* mentioned that he was so well acquainted with the 'Powers-that-be'. He now saw his old crony in a new light.

Archie was still sceptical.

"How come they're askin' *you* tae this top secret do?" he snapped. Tom shrugged.

"For ma expertise, Ah suppose," he sighed.

Archie wondered! The card looked authentic enough. He asked Tom to let him see the envelope, which he studied carefully before handing it grudgingly back.

"Aye, well," he said finally, "it's looks like ye're gonny have a wing-ding right enough, Tom!"

Archie's twinge of envy soon passed as the morning wore on. The invitation was the main topic of conversation and Archie and Sandy, caught up in the excitement of it all, suggested that they come round to Tom's place and keep him company on Christmas Eve.

But Tom was having none of it. This was *his* moment!

The rest of the week dragged in for Tom. He had taken his old Air Force uniform out of the wardrobe and, with reverent ceremony, had put it on. He was delighted it still fitted him after all these years…maybe just a *little* tight around the waist. He had sat for hours with a tin of Brasso and polished and buffed until the buttons sparkled and shone like twenty-four carat gold ducats. He lovingly pressed the blue tunic and pants, first with a damp tea towel and then with brown paper. He had managed to get rid of the smell of moth balls and, with a final brush of tunic and trousers on the ironing board, he replaced the uniform on a hanger and clipped it to the outside of the wardrobe door.

Tom stood back and surveyed his handiwork. He cleared the lump in his throat. His uniform was immaculate and he could have stepped on to any parade ground for inspection. He drew himself up to attention, puffed out his chest and gave a smart salute.

On Christmas Eve morning Tom was up with the lark. He was too excited for tea or toast. He gave himself a meticulous shave and blew away any overnight dust his ebony polished shoes might have gathered. Then it was into his uniform with the trousers edged razor-sharp. He sat down, careful not to crease his pants, and waited...and waited!

He sat, afraid to move, watching the mantleshelf clock. The hands seemed to be glued to the face and Tom wondered when his visitor or visitors would arrive...or if they *would* appear. The clock ticked on and the thought crossed his mind that perhaps the whole thing was an elaborate hoax. Could Archie and Sandy have set him up for a good laugh? Were they trying to teach him a lesson? He dismissed the thought almost immediately. They could never be so cruel!

Tom sat through most of the day...his eyes seldom leaving the clock on the shelf. As the night wore on his eyes became heavier and once in a while his head would fall forward as sleep enveloped him. He would jerk up, awake for a few moments until once again, drowsiness fell heavy on to him.

Once more it happened and it was the chimes of the old wall clock which brought him back with a start. Twelve o'clock midnight was striking. The old timepiece was five minutes fast and Christmas Eve would soon be Christmas Day.

Tom sighed and slowly rose from the chair. Someone had played a trick on him, he decided. He wondered who? Could it have been the postman? He stretched and yawned deeply. He would go to bed.

"Ach, well," he said to himself," it was a wee bit of excitement in ma life that Ah didnae expect. Nothin's been loast!"

He would be embarrassed telling Archie and Sandy how he'd been tricked. He didn't think they would laugh.

Tom removed his hat, breathed hard on the brass cap badge and polished it up with his sleeve. The uniform would go back into the wardrobe, probably never to be aired again.

The sudden, sharp knock on the door made him jump! It was a hard summons...an authorative rap! Tom slowly opened the door.

The two men, the elder in Air Force officer's uniform and the younger in the gear of an ordinary Aircraftsman, smiled. The officer held out his hand.

"Hello Tom," he said in greeting, "nice to meet you at last!" The younger man, too, pumped Tom's hand with a friendly grin. Tom's jaw fell and his head spun.

"I'm Mike," the officer said.

Tom flustered for a moment and then, remembering his manners, stammered:

"Er...come away in...er...sir...come in."

The two men entered and stood in the middle of the floor.

"You keep your place nice and tidy, Tom," the officer said.

Tom smiled.

"Aye, well ye dae yer best...Ah've nae wife, y'see."

The officer nodded.

"Yes, we know," he said.

Tom wondered *how* they knew. *He* didn't know them.

"Er...would youse like a wee cup o' tea!" he said.

The officer shook his head.

"Thanks anyway, Tom, but...er...no time. It's going to be a busy night!"

Tom scratched his head.

"Look," he said hesitantly, "Ah...er...really appreciate this wee surprise...but could ye tell me whit it's a' aboot?"

The two men laughed a hearty laugh!

"We've...er...been sent to fulfil your ambition, Tom...by a good friend of yours," the younger man said.

Suddenly it clicked with Tom. He snapped his fingers:

"Ah-Ah!" he exclaimed, "Ah know who did this...and who youse are."

"You do?" the younger man said, raising his eyebrows.

"Archie, wasn't it, eh? And youse two are frae the Flyin' Club in Cumbernauld, uren't youse?"

The officer shook his head.

"You've got it wrong, Tom."

Tom furrowed his brow.

"Well," he said, "Ah canny think who else it could be. Are youse here for tae take me on a wee flight...*THAT'S* ma greatest ambition, y'know...a wee flight!"

The officer nodded.

"Right first time, Tom!"

"Put on your helmet, Tom. Leave your cap here," the younger man said. Tom felt his legs go weak. He turned and rummaged excitedly in the drawer and came up with his flying helmet, which he placed on his head and strapped it firmly on.

"Where's yer aeroplane," he asked, trembling at the thought

that, at last, his great dream was about to be fulfilled. "Is it doon at Abbotsinch, eh...is it?"

The officer smiled:

"Who needs a plane, Tom!"

Suddenly there was a flash of brilliant lightning that illuminated the whole room in one blinding instant. Tom staggered back, his hand coming up to shield his eyes.

"Whit the Hell was that!" Tom gasped.

"Not Hell, Tom," the older man smiled.

When Tom's vision cleared his mouth gaped in disbelief. Gone were the two airforce men. His two visitors were completely transformed. The 'officer' was taller with long, blond shining hair that came down to his broad shoulders. He stood in a dazzling, white garment that reached his ankles. The younger man, too, stood radiant and resplendent. They smiled broadly.

Tom rubbed his eyes, stunned at by his encounter.

"Come along, Tom," the taller of the two said. "Your petition was heard...a very happy Christmas to you."

Each took hold of Tom's arms. He closed his eyes tightly as he felt a surge of mighty power and energy explode inside him. He felt his feet go away from under him and a rushing speed roar inside his ears. Suddenly the cold, night air stung at his face as he seemed to streak faster and faster with the dynamic power of a thunderbolt.

Hesitantly, and with some trepidation, he opened his eyes...and closed them again immediately as he saw the rooftops flash past underneath. He let out an involuntary yell of terror and only, gingerly, opened his eyes again when, there was no collision.

The two angels flew along beside him...one at either side. They had released his arms and he was flying solo...up, up and away. Farther and farther, he went, over the high buildings...

"YAHOO!" Tom cried with elation as he darted down lower and lower only to zoom up higher and higher with just the thought to power his intentions. He laughed excitedly as he did back flaps, victory rolls and looped the loop. He stretched out his arms, like wings, and growled like the Spitfire's engine...now and again spitting out imaginary bullets. Up over the hills, he flew! Down and down, skimming above the River Clyde's yellow ribbon as the moon winked and blinked and reflected on the dancing water.

They soared for hours below and above the clouds. Tom felt no chill as he weaved and ducked amongst the blue, shimmering stars.

"Time to go home now, Tom!"

Tom turned. The elder of his 'co-pilots' smiled and nodded towards the rooftops below. Tom closed his eyes as he felt himself dive faster and faster downwards until suddenly his feet felt solid ground beneath them. Slowly, he opened his eyes. He was back in his 'single end.' The two angels stood, each grinning from ear-to-ear.

"Well, Tom," the taller one said. "your prayer was answered!"

Tom suddenly felt very humble.

"Ye...er...ye mean *HE*...er...heard me when Ah...er...peyed a wee visit, eh?" he stuttered.

"HE hears *everybody*, Tom," the younger angel said.

Tom puckered his lip and sighed.

"And...er...whit's a' this aboot...you callin' yersel' Mike and a' this aboot an inauguration flight of Number Five."

The older angel laughed.

"It's right enough," he grinned. "I'm Michael, The Archangel, sometimes known as the Number One angel in the celestial hierarchy of Heavenly messengers. My colleague here," he said, nodding to the younger angel, "is Number Five...or he will be if *HE*," Michael pointed a thumb skywards, "decides he is worthy of his wings. *THIS* was his inauguration flight. *HE*, in his infinite wisdom, decided to kill two 'birds' with the one stone...you might say!"

Tom looked at the younger angel, who shuffled shyly.

"Ah hope ye've passed, son!" he said.

"He was nearly as good as you, Tom!" Michael grinned.

Tom blushed and, taking out his handkerchief, gave his nose a good blow.

"Who's...er...number Two, Three and Four top angels?" he said, knitting his brows.

"Well, Gabriel, of course, is Number Two and Raphael is Number Three, Number Four is...well...everybody's Guardian Angel, Tom" Michael said.

"Well, Ah just hope Number Five here has done a'right," Tom said, winking over at his young companion in flight.

"I'm sure he has," Michael said, "and you, too, Tom, have earned your wings. Here we are!"

Michael produced a pair of sparkling gold wings and ceremoniously pinned them to Tom's tunic.

"There you go!" he said, "Tom Brown, Pilot First Class!"

Tom flushed with a mixture of excitement and embarrassment.

"Aye...ye...er...sure youse widnae like a wee cup o' tea?" he stammered.

"No thanks, Tom," Michael said. "We've got to get going."

"No' even a wee *fly* cup?" Tom said with a twinkle.

The angels laughed.

"Sorry, Tom!" Michael said, "but we must go now. We'll see you again some day."

"Aye...er...sure," Tom said quietly ... "will ye ... er ... tell ... er ... *HIM*...er...thanks very much."

"You tell him, Tom," Michael said, "*YOU* tell him."

Before Tom could reply there was another blinding crash of lightning. Tom's arms came up, shielding his eyes as he turned away.

Suddenly he was in bed, lying staring at the ceiling. Sunshine flooded the room and he could hear the laughter and cries of the children in the street.

He rose and pulled back the curtain above the sink. Snow was lying thickly on the ground and the children were playing happily. Little girls pushed tiny prams, leaning over now and again to attend to the imaginary wails of hungry babies. Boys threw snowballs and pulled guns on hombres who needed guns pulled on them.

Tom smiled and let the curtain fall. He stepped in front of the fireplace and surveyed himself in the wall mirror. He was wearing his blue-striped pyjamas. He sighed, filled up the kettle and lit the gas ring. He would have a cup of tea!

So, it had all been a dream! But what a dream! He glanced at the wall clock – ten minutes to eleven. The Flying Duck would soon open its doors. Tom had slept longer than usual...but, he smiled to himself, it had been a hectic night!

He finished his tea and decided to wear his 'good suit' as it was Christmas morning. He opened the wardrobe door. His old uniform was where it was. But there was something extra there!

Pinned on the tunic was a bright, shining golden pair of wings! Tom, hands shaking drew the uniform out and held it up at arms length. The wings glistened in the morning sunshine streaming in the window. Tom hugged the tunic to his chest and flopped down on the easy chair. It wasn't a dream after all! He brushed the tear from the corner of his eye, brought out his 'good suit' and was soon standing in front of the wall mirror, clean and as bright as a button...or a pair of wings, and smelling sweetly from a good splash of after shave lotion.

He put the wings into his inside pocket, let his eyes sweep the room...in case he had any unexpected visitors, and stepped out, locking the door behind him. He made on important call on his. way to The Flying Duck! The church was full for the morning service and Tom slid into a pew at the back. He enjoyed the young minister's sermon...about the Nativity and how the angels appeared to the shepherds in the hills. They're a busy lot, these angels, Tom thought to himself.

The service over, Tom got up, turned at the door and gave a 'thumbs-up'. "Thanks, again!" he said silently and stepped out into the crisp, fresh morning.

Archie and Sandy were already at their usual table by the window. Tom ambled over.

"Merry Christmas, lads!" he said smiling broadly. Archie and Sandy took his outstretched hand and wished him the compliments of the season. Tom sat down and immediately Jimmy, the barman, was over with three pints of frothy lager.

"Merry Christmas, boys," he said cheerily. "On the house," he added, nodding towards the drinks.

The happy trio beamed and uttered grateful thanks. They clinked glasses, wished each other seasonal greetings once more and sipped slowly.

"Well?" Archie said at last.

"Well whit?" Tom asked, a rougish grin on his face.

"Well, whit happened?" Archie cried with impatience.

"How did you get on?" Sandy said, leaning over expectantly.

"Oh, fine...just fine," Tom said, deliberately irritating his friends.

Archie threw up his arms.

"Are ye gonny tell us or no'?" he said, gritting his teeth. "Did ye go on this inauguration flight...this number Five or whitever it was?"

Tom nodded.

"Ah did," he said. "It was marvellous, so it was!"

Tom proudly pulled out his golden wings.

"Look," he said, smiling broadly, "they presented me wi' these."

Archie took the wings and studied them with awe, passing them over to Sandy, who looked at Tom in a new light and with great admiration.

Archie clicked his tongue and said:

"Ah must admit, Tom, Ah didnae believe a word o' anythin' ye said. No' that ye're a liar, mind ye – just that ye're imaginative, know whit Ah mean?"

"Aye, ye're a Biggles, Tom – right oot the comics," Sandy giggled.

"Aye, a fly midden," Archie laughed.

Tom grinned.

"Wi the emphasis oan 'fly', eh?" he said.

Archie nodded and smiled.

"Aye...and who cares if a' yer stories are a loat o'baloney? Ye keep us goin', Tom. And ye'll have tae tell us a' aboot this latest adventure o' yours, eh?"

"Oh, aye, ye will!" Sandy said seriously.

"Aye, but let's have oor beer first. It's been some Christmas!, aye, some Christmas!" Tom said, with a faraway look.

The three men raised their glasses.

"A merry Christmas tae everybody," they chorused.

Tom nodded:

"Aye, a very Christmas and especially tae aviators everywhere, eh?"

Archie and Sandy concurred.

"Tae them a'!" they echoed.

Tom smiled, took a long swig of his drink, wiped his mouth with his cuff and looked through the window. He looked up at the cloudless sky and gave a thumbs-up.

"Tae them a'," he repeated, "and tae two especially...Angels One Five!"

The Old Lag

Old Jimmy Hunter stood up and let his eyes sweep round his cell. This was his home for the past twenty-two years and he had to admit that his 'apartment', in Glasgow's Barlinnie Jail, was neater than some of the seaside boarding houses he had graced.

On the wall, a coloured picture, torn from a magazine, gorgeous Betty Grable, smiled down with polished pearl teeth...and beautiful Rita Hayworth and Jimmy Cagney and, not forgetting, *SANTA CLAUS!*

Jimmy rubbed his hands together and did a gleeful hop, skip and jump! Christmas was near and hadn't he been voted the best Santa Claus ever to enter the Christmas Day dining hall with a legitimate sackfull of swag?

It was the greatest day of the year for Old Jimmy and one he looked forward to the minute the tinsel was packed away until the next time.

He had already arranged with Mr Watts, the governor, to have the bright-red Santa costume unpacked and unmothballed.

He crossed the cell, looked at himself in the wall mirror and nodded, satisfied. His six-month growth of beard had reached the regulation Santa Claus length and was silver-white as approved by a worldful of hopeful children!

"Jimmy, Mr Watts wants to see ye!" The warder turned on his heels and Jimmy shuffled after him. Maybe they've bought a new costume at last, he thought! The old one was as tattered as himself.

Mr Watts rose the minute Jimmy entered the office.

"Jimmy," he beamed, coming round from his desk with outstretched hand, "great news! You're being released next Tuesday...how aboot that then eh?"

Jimmy's jaw dropped as Mr Watts energetically pumped his hand.

"Bu...bu...but Ah don't want tae be released," he stammered.

"This is ma home, Mr Watts…the only hame Ah've ever known! Ah'd be loast oot there!"

Mr Watts bit his lip…he understood.

"Aw, Jimmy," he sighed, "I know how ye feel…but it's the rules. There's nothing I can do. The Parole Board say that you've done your time and you've to be freed to live the rest of yer life in peace."

"Bu…but who'll be Santa Claus this year?" Jimmy said softly. "Ah mean ma fellow colleagues here *expect* me tae be there on Christmas moarnin'. Ah mean, Ah'm Santa, Mr Watts, Ah am Santa…they expect it so they dae!"

"I'm sorry, Jimmy," Mr Watts said turning away.

The tall warder took Jimmy by the arm and gently steered him towards the door.

"Whit aboot ma Christmas dinner," the old lag said, turning. "Ah'm entitled tae that, surely?"

Mr Watts did not look up and Jimmy, head bowed, shuffled towards his cell.

Tuesday arrived and Mr McKenzie, the warder, shook Jimmy's hand and led him along the passageway. Fellow inmates shouted and whistled as Jimmy, tear in eye, waved back.

The huge gate swung open and, with a final handshake from Mr Mckenzie, Jimmy stepped out and into freedom.

There was nobody there to greet him. Jimmy's family were all behind that wall. Every prisoner his son!

Jimmy booked himself into a working men's hostel and was allocated a small room, sparsely furnished. Not a patch on his Barlinnie cell, he decided. He began to make it as homely as possible. Betty Grable, Rita Hayworth, Jimmy Cagney…and Santa Claus were soon pinned to the wall.

Jimmy sat at the edge of his bed and put his head in his hands.

"Well, now…what's all the despair, friend, eh?"

Jimmy looked up. The man standing at his door was a big man, round as a barrel and had a wide, cheery grin. His voice boomed!

"Why the gloom, eh?" It'll soon be Christmas…a time of joy and laughter!"

"Aye, maybe for you," Jimmy snapped, he didn't appreciate this jollity when he was down. "Ye call this a place of laughter an' joy? he said.

The big man was suddenly serious.

"It could be worse!" he said. "Just think of all the folk who don't have a bed this night...who sleep in cardboard boxes in the street."

Jimmy thought for a moment and finally nodded.

"Ah suppose ye're right!" he agreed.

"Still, Ah miss ma auld hame...the camaraderie an' a' that...know whit Ah mean, pal?"

"Where was that, then?" the big man asked.

"Barlinnie Jail," Jimmy replied, almost with reverence. "Aye, Ah was there for mair than twenty years, Ah was!"

"You must've done something pretty serious to have a sentence like that slapped on you!" the stranger said with almost a reprimand.

Jimmy shook his head.

"No' really," he said, "Ah was jist tryin' tae make a few bob...tae make ends meet, know whit Ah mean?"

"You robbed a bank?" the big man asked, his eyes narrowing.

"Naw, naw," Jimmy said quickly. "Ah...er...did a wee bit printin'...a wee bit o' forgery an' that...Jist enough tae keep the wolf frae the door. Even the heid man at the bank said ma fivers was the best he'd ever seen." Jimmy puffed out his chest.

The man came into the room, closing the door behind him, and joined Jimmy at the edge of the bed.

"How much did you...er...make?" he quizzed.

"A hundred thousand," Jimmy said with a hint of pride.

The big man nodded.

"Aye, I suppose *that* deserves twenty years!" he exclaimed.

"Mind ye, Ah gave maist o' it away," Jimmy was quick to point out. "Tae pensioners maistly," he went on. "Still, that didnae cut any ice wi' the judge. He said Ah was a menace tae society and could cause ructions wi' the country's economy. They've nae heart, they judges, so they've no'!"

"Well, you're free now to get on with the rest of your life," the man said quietly.

"Aye, wi' nae faimily!", Jimmy said softly. "A' ma faimily are still inside. Ah was their Santy Claus, y'know," he went on, perking up. "Every Christmas Ah donned the gear and it was marvellous, so it was!"

Jimmy brushed his eye with the back of his hand.

"You'll miss it this year, then, eh?" the stranger said.

Jimmy nodded:

"Aye, Ah will," he said in a whisper.

The Big Man slapped him on the back and guffawed.

"Well," he cried, "You'll just have to go back inside and do your duty, eh!"

Jimmy shook his head.

"It's no' as easy as that!" he said. "It's the rules...the governor telt me. Ye canny break the rules, he said."

"You won't *be* breaking the rules if you're *sent* back," the stranger said.

Jimmy's eyebrows shot up.

"Whit dae ye mean?" he said suspiciously.

"Just go out and rob a bank and they'll soon have you inside again!" the man said nonchalantly. He rose, walked to the door and turned. "Just you think about it," he said and left, grinning from ear-to-ear.

Jimmy sat silent for a moment and then a twinkle came to his eye. The big fella's right he thought. Why hadn't he thought of this before?

He fell back on the bed, cradled his head in his cupped hands, and closed his eyes.

Jimmy fell into a deep sleep and awoke, startled by the clanging of bells in his ears.

He was elated for a moment, thinking he was hearing a bank's alarm and that he would soon be caught, firmly grabbed by security men. He sighed when he saw the ear-piercing ringing came from his portable alarm clock. Eight thirty in the morning! He rose, washed himself and made his way down to the dining hall.

Soon he was sipping a steaming hot mug of sweet tea. He looked around. There was no sign of the Big Man and Jimmy reckoned that he had got up early and had left for work. He hoped he would see him later in the evening.

Jimmy stepped out into the chill morning air. He would walk around and take in the sights. A thin powder of snow lay on the pavements and Jimmy wrapped his woollen scarf tightly around his neck. The town had changed since his stay at Barlinnie.

Buildings had been pulled down and others were in their place. He noted, with some satisfaction, that there were more banks around than the old days. Yes, a good choice there! The biggest bank was at the corner and Jimmy was pleased to note that two policemen were standing chatting just outside its doors.

As well to get started on his robbing mission and there was no time like the present, he reckoned.

Jimmy smiled at the policemen as he squeezed past and entered the bank.

He made his way to a counter, took a piece of paper from a slot and, taking the ball-point pen from its screwed down stand, tapped his cheek and thought deeply. Ah! He decided what to write!

"This is a hold-up. Put all the money into a paper bag and keep your mouth shut or you will be blasted to kingdom come!"

Jimmy read his note over and over and was satisfied. He stood in the shortest queue and was soon facing the smiling young girl teller.

Quietly he slipped the note over and waited for her horrified reaction.

The girl read the note, looked up at Jimmy and giggled.

"Just hang on a minute, sir," she said and walked off with Jimmy's note clutched in her hand.

Jimmy watched as she approached an obvious senior clerk who had his own desk at the back. He saw the girl hand him the note, turn and point to Jimmy, whose eyes had narrowed in mock menace.

The senior clerk smiled, rose and followed the girl as they went around the other tellers and clerks...each time pointing to bewildered Jimmy.

They all smiled at Jimmy and some even gave him a 'Thumbs-Up' sign. The girls came back and handed Jimmy a paper bag that jingled.

"Happy Christmas!" she smiled.

Jimmy shuffled towards the door, stunned. Stepping out into the street, he stopped and began to count his 'haul'.

"Hello, hello," the taller of the two policemen said, approaching him. "Ye did all right there, eh?"

Jimmy screwed up his eyebrows.

"Are ye kiddin'?" he cried. "Two pounds an' fifty-pence...sheer robbery, so it is!"

The policeman laughed and dug into his pocket.

"Here," he said, "a wee bit extra," and he popped fifty pence into Jimmy's hand. His colleague came over and did likewise.

"A Merry Christmas Old Timer," they said in unison and walked off up in the street.

Jimmy wondered how they knew he was an 'Old Timer?'

Jimmy had reckoned at least on twenty-thousand pounds for his hold-up. He read and re-read his demand note and decided that banks nowadays were employing illiterates! That girl obviously couldn't read...and that went for the senior clerk as well!

He definitely had *not* written, 'Wull you put the hat roon' for me?'

At dinner time, Jimmy was back in the hostel's dining room enjoying the pleasure of a pie and chips.

"Ah, there you are!" The big stranger's voice boomed round the room. "Mind if I join you?"

He didn't wait for an answer and sat down alongside Jimmy.

"Well," he inquired, "how did it go?"

Jimmy shook his head.

"Ah don't understaun' it," he said, explaining the day's events.

The big man let out a roar and slapped his thigh in glee.

"Well, you'll just have to keep trying," he roared.

Jimmy nodded. "Ah suppose so!" he said.

Next morning Jimmy decided to have another go. After a quick breakfast, he caught a bus and headed into town. He would try another bank...a bank where the workers knew how to read. Jimmy had re-written his note: 'This is a stick-up. I have a gun. Put the money in this bag...or else'.

He smiled, satisfied that nothing would go wrong this time.

Jimmy would try a smaller bank this time. He popped into a few of the High Street building societies and banks and finally selected a small but busy bank on the main road.

He stood back for a moment and, scanning the faces of the tellers, selected a grumpy looking middle-aged teller who never smiled and whose mouth turned down at the corners. Now and then he would flick his moustache with a deft finger. Yes, Jimmy thought, this bloke would stand no nonsense!

Jimmy stood in the queue and was soon face-to-face with 'Auld Grumpy'.

Quickly, he slipped the note over. The wee man took the note, peered over the top of his pince-nez...and smiled broadly.

"Wonderful! Wonderful!" he exclaimed. "Look...everybody look"... he cried. And everyone behind the grill hurried over and peered at Jimmy's note.

Everyone started digging into their pockets and thrusting money into Jimmy's paper bag.

"Good luck to you...and a Merry Christmas," Grumpy chuckled.

Everyone began to applaud and the Security Man, after depositing a pound coin into the bag, ushered Jimmy to the door.

"A Happy Yuletide," he called as, once more, Jimmy found himself out in the street.

Jimmy sat dumped at the dinner table that night.

"You still here?" the Big Man said, flopping down on the opposite seat.

Once more Jimmy recounted the day's tragic events. The man roared with laughter...his booming voice making other residents slap palms over their cups to stop spillage.

Jimmy wasted no time the next day. He marched into the nearest bustling bank, walked straight up to the elderly woman teller and shoved the prepared note across.

The woman picked up the note, let her eyes scan the words and let out a piercing shriek...of delight!

Jimmy threw up his arms in despair.

"Aw, forget it!" he snapped and, turning, he walked out with the happy chorus of 'Merry Christmas' echoing in his ears.

Jimmy stood on the pavement and scratched his puzzled head. An old lady passing stopped and thrust a five pound note into his hand wishing him seasonal greetings.

Back at the hostel Jimmy counted up the money he had gathered over the past days. There was almost a hundred pounds there! Not bad, he thought for a botched up effort. He put the cash into an old purse and hid it in a sock which he put with the rest of his underwear in a corner of a drawer.

It was Christmas Eve and Jimmy was joined at the dinner table by his new friend, who, when hearing his tale of woe, commiserated with him.

"The moarra's Christmas Day," Jimmy said sadly, "an' they'll have another Santa at Barlinnie...but it'll no' be the same! Ah mean it was expected o' me tae be there...Ah had ma fans, y'know," he added proudly.

The Big Man stood up and patted Jimmy on the shoulder.

"Never say die!" he said and left Jimmy gazing into his tea.

Jimmy awoke next day to the sound of bells from a nearby church. Christmas Day!

He took his time getting up and lay thinking of what was going on at the 'Bar-L'. They'd be having breakfast right now, he reckoned. He sighed and swung his feet on to the cold linoleumed floor.

He would go out, find a small inexpensive restaurant and treat himself to a turkey and chestnut stuffing dinner. He'd purchase a paper hat and some Christmas crackers and would find a quiet corner and eat...alone!

He washed and dressed and rummaged around the drawer for his sock containing the week's 'booty'. He found the sock...and the money gone!

Frantically, he started pulling everything out of the drawer, searching every sock and every pocket. He went through his trouser and jacket pockets...but all to no avail!

He slumped on to the edge of the bed and, in despair, shook his head. He took out his wallet from his hip pocket and peered inside. Turning it upside down, a slip of paper fluttered to the floor.

Jimmy's brows knitted as he picked it up:

"Thanks for the cash, old friend," the note said. "I'll see it goes to good use. Your Big Pal."

Jimmy was stunned. Who would have thought that the big, jolly stranger with the booming laugh would turn out to be a better candidate for Barlinnie than he was? You just can't trust anybody these days, he thought with disgust!

Jimmy checked with the hostel supervisor.

"The Big Fella checked out last night," the man said coldly.

Jimmy wrapped up and stepped out into the street. Thick snow was falling heavily now and he turned up the collar of his overcoat and headed down towards the town centre. Being Christmas morning, traffic was light and Jimmy didn't notice the police car pass him by, stop and turn, and follow him. The car pulled up a few yards ahead.

"You there," a voice bellowed from the car's open window.

Jimmy went over.

Mr McKenzie, the warder, stepped from the car.

"Jimmy," he said, offering his outstretched hand. "A Merry Christmas tae ye auld son. We've been lookin' for ye everywhere! The man at the hostel said ye had just left."

"Whit were ye lookin' for me for?" Jimmy asked, puckering his eyebrows.

"Mr Watts wants tae see ye," Mr McKenzie said leaning over and opening the back door. "C'mon, get in."

Jimmy climbed into the back of the police car, enjoying the warmth that enveloped him.

"Whit does he want *me* for, Mr McKenzie?"

Mr McKenzie shrugged. "Don't know, Jimmy. He just told me tae fetch you!"

Jimmy wondered how Mr Watts knew his address but shrugged it off. 'Polis and high heid yins know these things', he reckoned.

"Gonny put yeer siren oan Mr Polis?" Jimmy asked boyishly. The police driver smiled and flicked on the wailing siren as they headed for the Bar-L. Jimmy leaned back and enjoyed the thrill...remembering the old days!

"Ye'll be a' set for yer Christmas dinner, eh?" Jimmy said.

Mr McKenzie nodded:

"Aye, everything's well in hand, Jimmy. And whit have *you* been daein' wi' yersel'...forby playin' Santa?"

Jimmy's eyebrows shot up.

"Whit dae ye mean, 'Playin' Santa'?"

"A' they banks ye've been goin' roon'...dressed up as Faither Christmas and collectin' for Prisoners' Aid and the toon's down-an-outs, eh! It was a nice thought, Jimmy...and Mr Watts was delighted wi' that money ye sent in for the Christmas treat – nearly a hundred pounds, eh! A nice wee haul, Jimmy!"

Jimmy stared blankly ahead. The Big Man must have sent it on his behalf. He smiled to himself. He always *knew* there was something just nice and honest aboot that Jolly Big Giant!

"Aye, an' the poetry, tae, eh?" Mr McKenzie went on.

"Whit poetry was that?" Jimmy quizzed.

"The notes ye haunded the bank clerks...like this..."

Mr McKenzie produced a note from his tunic pocket and, clearning his throat, began to read.

"The World's Greatest Saver would like to make a wee withdrawal...for the less fortunate!...See", he said handing Jimmy the note. "And the wee drawin' of the wee babe in a manger in the stable gave it that wee bit o' class...poetic...for *HE* was the world's saver!"

Jimmy sat in silence. He could hear Mr McKenzie's voice echoing somewhere in the distance.

"And every bank clerk that saw ye agreed that you were the best ever Santa Claus they'd ever seen," he went on. "Magnificent was the word they used."

The police car swung through the massive gates of Barlinnie Prison and Mr McKenzie ushered an incredulous Jimmy through to the office of Mr Watts who met him with outstretched hand.

"Jimmy," he said, pumping his hand as only Mr Watts knew how to pump hands, "I don't know how to thank you. Your money came in an anonymous letter saying it was being forwarded on your behalf and it was to be divided between the Prisoners' Aid Society and the town's homeless. And that you had collected the money going round the banks in your favourite guise of Father Christmas..."

"Well...er..." Jimmy stammered "Ah...er...didnae really...er..."

"Say no more, Jimmy," Mr Watts interrupted. "Now, in recognition of your great charitable heart, I would be grateful if you would agree to be our Santa Claus once more, Jimmy, and stay for Christmas dinner with us...what do you say?"

Jimmy wiped the tears from his eyes and pride swelled up in his heart.

"Well...er...if ye really think Ah could..."

He didn't get finishing. Mr Watts took his arm.

"C'mon," he said, "let's get you ready!" Mr McKenzie had already brought out the Santa Claus costume which he handed over to Jimmy, not saying anything.

Jimmy let his hands run down the rough, wonderful cloth and held it for a moment to his cheek. He fluffed up his beard and swung the bag of goodies across his shoulder.

"Right," he said at last, "Ah'm ready, Mr Watts."

Jimmy proudly led the way...along the corridor and down the stairs. The dining room doors swung open and a warder at each side saluted smartly. Jimmy braced himself and stepped through. A single pair of hands began to applaud and then another and another as the old timers recognised their favourite Santa. Soon the hall resounded to thunderous clapping and whistling.

Jimmy's chest expanded to full capacity.

Everybody stood up and the hall erupted into a crescendo of 'For He's a Jolly Good Fellow!' His old mates shook his hand warmly as he dug into the bag and distributed the presents.

Afterwards there was the big tuck in.

"Well, Jimmy," Mr Watts said when it was all over, "just for you there's a special dispensation. You can have your old cell...just for tonight."

Mr Watts and Mr McKenzie escorted Jimmy to his old home and shook his hands.

"Merry Christmas, Jimmy," they echoed, 'Sleep well!'"

Jimmy sniffed and entered the cell. On the wall were torn-edged pictures of Betty Grable and Rita Hayworth and Jimmy Cagney. "The best we could find, Jimmy...MERRY CHRISTMAS – from yer auld chinas!" the pinned-up note said.

Old Jimmy wiped his eyes with the rough cuff of his sleeve and lay down on top of his bunk.

All was quiet now with the still of the night broken only by the echoing footsteps of the patrolling warders.

He closed his eyes and wondered about the big stranger? *HE* would have made a good Santa Claus himself, he thought. Yes, he wondered about him!

Jimmy was drifting off to sleep when suddenly he opened his eyes with a start.

"MERRY CHRISTMAS, JIMMY!" the voice boomed – "AND A HAPPY NEW YEAR!...HO-HO-HO."

Jimmy smiled! He had heard that loud, jolly laugh before.

Maggie

Sister McKenzie stepped down from the ladder, stood back and surveyed her work. She smiled with satisfaction. "There, how does it look?" she said.

The residents of Resthaven Home for the Elderly broke into rapturous applause. The Christmas tree was beautiful! It brought back happy memories of childhood.

The cars would be arriving anytime now to whisk them off for their Christmas Eve treat...the pantomime at the local church hall.

This was a hardy annual for the old folks! Everyone looked forward to it with great anticipation...well, *almost* everyone.

Old Maggie was surely...a loner! She never took part in any of the Home's activities. She seldom spoke...unless to complain. And now, she sat by the window and watched the gleaming cars sweep up the driveway, horns honking. The happy residents, decked out in paper hats, chatted and laughed loudly as they spilled out and were helped into the cars by kindly volunteers. The doors slammed and Maggie watched as the red tail lights vanished round the bend on the pathway.

The room suddenly silent Maggie took out a handkerchief and dabbed her tired eyes and blew her nose. She was ninety-four now and the longest serving guest at the Home.

She had been there for twenty-eight years...arriving just two years after Tom died. Tom and Maggie had never been blessed with a family!

She never had a visitor or received mail. Birthdays came and went...never a card! Only the nurses at the Home put on a little show, with a cake and candles. And, even then, Maggie grumbled.

Maggie rose from her chair as the last car vanished. She hobbled off to her room and her solitude.

The cars were back in on time and the happy, noisy revellers jostled into the drawing room amid a babble of conversation.

The chatter stopped suddenly as Maggie stepped in carrying a large handbag. She wore a natty straw hat with artificial cherries on top...and was smiling at everyone.

"Hope you all had a lovely time," she cooed and headed for her favourite seat by the window.

Everyone gasped! Maggie eased herself into the large moquette chair, opened her bag and produced knitting needles, a large ball of blue wool and an almost finished scarf.

The clickety-clack of her needles echoed round the hushed room. Then the chatter started up again...and Maggie's transformation was the topic of conversation.

Maggie clicked on, a large smile on her craggy face.

"Why Maggie, you're looking wonderful!" Sister McKenzie said. Maggie nodded.

"Have tae look ma best for ma visitor!" she smiled.

"Your visitor?" Sister McKenzie's eyebrows rose.

"And why should Ah no' have a visitor?" Maggie snapped, forgetting herself.

"Oh, no reason," Sister McKenzie said quickly, "But...er...you don't usually have a visitor," she added cautiously.

Maggie didn't look up. Her needle clicked on to the end of the row. She held up the blue, woollen scarf at arms length.

"There...whit dae ye think o' it?" she smiled. "Dae ye think he'll like it?"

"It's lovely, Maggie," Sister McKenzie said, feeling the soft, warm wool. "But...er...who is it for?" she said softly.

"It's for ma godson," Maggie replied, casting an approving glance over her handiwork.

"I didn't know you had a godson, Maggie," Sister McKenzie said with surprise. "You never mentioned him before."

"Did Ah no'?" Maggie smiled.

"Well, he's never written or inquired about you, Maggie," the sister said, a little annoyed. "Surely he could've"...Maggie held up her hand.

"He's a busy feller," she said, "an' has mair tae dae than bother aboot an' auld thing like me."

"But surely..." Sister McKenzie started, but was stopped by Maggie's raised hand once again.

"The main thing is that he's comin' tae see me the night...he telt me. This scarf is a wee present Ah meant for his birthday last year...but he couldnae manage then. So, it'll dae this year!"

Sister McKenzie smiled. She knew it was all in Maggie's mind but would humour her and leave her to her dreams.

"Dae ye think he'll like the scarf, Sister?" Maggie asked hopefully.

"How could he not, Maggie...it's beautiful!" Maggie nodded.

"Aye, Ah'm lucky that ma fingers can still haud a knittin' needle at ma age!" she exclaimed.

After supper and bedtime had come round, the residents headed for their rooms...and bed. Maggie didn't stir.

"Maggie, it's time for bed," Sister McKenzie said softly.

"Let me sit just a while longer," the old lady said, a plea in her eye. "He's maybe been held up...he's a busy feller, y'know!" Sister McKenzie smiled and kissed Maggie's cheek.

"Just a wee while, then," she said.

Maggie had rolled up the ball of wool and replaced it in her bag. The scarf was neatly folded and resting on her lap.

Sister McKenzie looked back and saw the old lady close her eyes, a large smile on her face. She closed the door quietly and left her to her thoughts.

She felt pity that Maggie would be disappointed once more. The old lady's godson hadn't come last year...or any other year.

On the stroke of midnight the church bells in the small town began to ring. Snow fluttered down and left a soft white carpet. The trees in the grounds of Resthaven Home for the Elderly glistened a frosty sparkle as the falling snow enveloped their green, winter leaves.

Carols echoed up from the church choir..."Away in a Manger, no crib for a bed..."

Sister McKenzie had done her rounds. The guests were sound asleep in *their* beds. She silently opened the drawing room door. Maggie, eyes closed and still with that happy smile, had not moved.

Quietly, Sister McKenzie approached the old lady. She knew at once that Maggie had gone.

Her hand came up to her mouth to stifle a gasp. The blue woollen scarf, too, had gone. Her eyes widened. Grasped in Maggie's clenched hand was...a thorn!

Tears welled up in Sister McKenzie's eyes. But they were tears of happiness for Old Maggie...

A young nurse came in. She saw the wetness in Sister McKenzie's eyes.

"Maggie's gone?" she asked.

Sister McKenzie nodded.

The young nurse sighed:

"She was looking forward so much to her godson coming to visit her, too!" she said softly, "even though it was just a dream."

Sister McKenzie wiped her eyes and smiled.

"Yes," she said quietly, "but He *DID* come...He had to come for the lovely birthday present Maggie knitted for him – the one she's been waiting a year to give him..."

"I thought she had just dreamed up a godson...as an excuse for knitting that scarf," the nurse said.

Sister McKenzie shook her head:

"No, she didn't dream him up," she whispered. "He *DID* visit her tonight for his little present This was the FOURTH gift he received on the day of his birth..."

"You mean...you mea...?

The young nurse didn't get finishing the sentence. Sister McKenzie nodded.

"Yes," she said, "and He really was her GOD'S SON!"

Taking The Michael

St Michael's Isle lay twenty two miles out in the Atlantic Ocean off Scotland's north-west coast. Time had passed the island by and its presence was not generally known to the wide world. Not that the seven hundred or so islanders particularly cared. They got on with earning their living...mostly by fishing the teeming waters or sheep farming in the lush hills!

Gossip was usually about the weather and the current highlight was that Miss Jeannie McPherson was pregnant...again!

Pride of the island was the centuries old grey-stoned church which stood at the top of the hill and was dedicated to the great St. Michael the Archangel himself. The island was so far out of the way that even the 16th century Reformation had ignored it.

The old church was built from locally quarried stone and could be seen clearly from McDougall's pub, which was just across the main street at the foot of the hill.

It was there that the Parish Council would meet on the first Friday of each month and discuss important issues such as the rising price of votive candles, or the purchase of a new pair of shoes for the parish priest, Father Hamish McGinty.

Felix Urquhart was a regular member of the council and was known to attend these meetings with some sobriety...but only just!

The small, elderly Felix, would stagger from the hostelry, cross the road and lurch his way up the hill to the church, where he would light a candle for the repose of the soul of his dear mother and crash to his knees in solemn, if not slurred, prayer.

When he had finished, he would stumble to his feet, take a deep breath and genuflect as best he could...although sometimes it took a good fifteen minutes for him to get to his feet again. Then, pulling his waistcoat down at the front and with as straight a gait as he could muster, he would leave the church and stagger down the hill and right into McDougall's once more.

It was on one of these Friday nights that the tranquility of St Michael's Isle was shattered forever by an event that would make headlines all over the world.

The Parish Council met as usual that night. Father McGinty complained, as usual, about the previous Sunday's takings in the plate. In fact even the plate was taken, he moaned.

Wullie Thomson, the treasurer, sympathised but said nothing could be done to swell the parish coffers. The only swelling on the island was coming from Miss Jeannie McPherson. The group sat morosely sipping their drinks and Wullie ambled over to the window, pint in hand, and, pulling the curtain back, peered into the night. He caught sight of old Felix, who had been in the pub earlier, staggering up the hill on his weekly pilgrimage.

"There goes auld Felix," Wullie murmured, sipping his pint, "Ye would think his auld maw would be oot o' Purgatory by this time! She's been deid aboot four hunner' years!"

Father McGinty rebuked Wullie's insensitivity, saying Auld Missus Urquhart could not have expired any more than two hundred years ago. A titter went round the group.

"Only the Good Lord Himsel' can decide when ye're time in Purgatory is finished," he declared solemnly, adding, "He's the wan that says when the Holy Souls can get oot o' the Holy Coals."

Wullie spluttered on his drink!

Felix had arrived at the church as usual and staggered down the centre aisle. He dug deeply into his pocket and finally produced a coin and, with great fumbling, managed to get it into the slot for the purchase of a votive candle. Striking a match, after staggering backwards a couple of times, he leaned over to light the candle...and lost his balance. The lighted match flew from his hand and landed on the white linen altar cloth. Within seconds the crisp, dry altar cloth was ablaze...with the licking flames running across the entire width of the main altar. From there it caught on to the candles at the far side and burst into flaming life like an exploding bomb. Felix stared, stunned as the flames raged and the candles spluttered and sent flaming darts in every direction. The fire swept upwards, towards the dry, oak beams that spanned the church. Within seconds the crackling wood spat out orange-hot cinders on to the wooden pews below. The hungry flames licked rapidly at the old, worn seats and shot across the width of the entire church.

Felix staggered to his feet, completely sobered now, and hurried towards the exit...dodging raining embers as best he could. At the main door he stopped, turned and did a quick genuflection ...muttering an apology.

Wullie Thomson, still standing at McDougall's window, stared in disbelief! The night sky above the church was tinged crimson and huge, yellow and red raging flames spat out and up into the air. He turned to Father McGinty, who was now on the sad subject of Jeannie McPherson.

"Fa...Fa...Father," Wullie stuttered, "the ch...church is oan fire!"

Father McGinty and the rest of the group were momentarily stunned at this terrible observation but soon quickly moved into action. Led by the good priest, they threw back their chairs - making sure not a drop was spilled - and hurried over to the window. And there they stood, and, mouths drooping, they gawked at the dire sight before them.

St Michael's was a raging inferno...hell on the hill!

"Ah'll bet Auld Felix did it!" Wullie volunteered.

"No' deliberately!" McDougall, the barrell-shaped publican, said, shaking his head. "He widnae blackmail the Almighty like that...'Let ma maw oot o' Purgatory or Ah'll set yer chapel oan fire...naw, it's no' in Felix tae dae that!"

"Ah'm no' sayin' he would dae it deliberately," Wullie retorted, "It could've been an accident! Ah mean, look at the way he staggers up there every Friday! An' he stammers an' slurs...and it's a wonder that God understaun's whit he's bloody talkin' aboot."

Father McGinty said nothing. He was too shocked. Blindly, he left the pub and, staring blankly ahead, crossed the road and walked up the hill towards the blazing church building. There was no need to hurry. There was nothing to be done. He looked Heavenwards:

"Why? Why noo?" he said with a slight whimper. "Why noo...this minute...jist wan week efter the insurance ran oot. Ah've got nothin' tae re-build it...no' a curdy! An' there's nae point askin' them...they've nae money either. They even pinch the bloo...the plates."

He shook his head and wearily carried on up the hill. The entire town had turned out and had climbed up the steep hill...all, except Jeannie McPherson.

The cold, grey daylight was a long time in coming. But they stayed there beside their smouldering church. Only the solid, sturdy stone shell now stood atop the hill...like a monument. Old women wrapped their woollen shawls tightly around their trembling, frail bodies and dabbed their tear-stained eyes.

Felix was beside himself with remorse and had to run the gauntlet of verbal abuse. But Father McGinty had put a comforting arm around his shoulder and, in true Christian fashion, had told him not to worry and that there was a purpose for everything. "Although," he went on, "Ah'm damned if Ah know whit it is here!"

Father McGinty had been summoned to the mainland and an encounter with the Bishop.

He was rapped for allowing the church's insurance to run out and was advised by his stern, but not unsympathetic, bishop that the archdiocese could not help. Father McGinty would have to raise the money himself.

When the good priest returned from his meeting the council was hurriedly summoned and the bad news relayed...The men sat down in silence, only the slow sipping of their drinks broke the heavy quietness.

"Anybody got any ideas?" Father McGinty said hopefully.

There was no response. They sat, staring into their glasses until finally Wullie Thomson snapped his fingers and sat bolt upright with a water-melon grin on his face.

"How aboot askin' everybody in the toon tae chip in a pound apiece and we could put it a' on lottery tickets? We could win millions!"

His bright idea was shot down by Erchie Campbell, the town's undertaker.

"Get a pound aff folk who steal the bloody collection plates...nae chance!" he snarled.

Felix, who had been uncharacteristically quiet, spoke up:

"If...if only we had a tourist trade!" he volunteered. "Them holidaymakers bring in stacks o' cash tae wee places like this, so they dae!"

"An' where would we bloody put them?" Erchie Campbell sneered.

"Auld Granny Gorman used tae take in boarders," Wullie ventured.

"Aw, that's great, that is!" Erchie retorted, throwing up his arms. "Can ye imagine sayin' tae the auld sowel...'dae ye mind if we stick four hunner tourists in yer back bedroom?"

McDougall thought the idea of a tourist trade was a good one...but not practical in their particular circumstances.

"There's nothin' here for tourists," he said seriously. "Ye must have an attraction, that's whit ye need...an attraction."

"It's a bloody miracle we need," Wullie Thomson piped up, "that's whit we bloody need...a miracle!"

Felix agreed:

"Ah wance read a book aboot Lourdes, that's in...er..."

"France, Felix...France," Father McGinty said, coming to his aid.

"Aye, France," Felix agreed. "An' the Virgin Mary hersel' appeared there tae a wee lassie called...er...Bert..."

"Bernadette," Father McGinty corrected, "Bernadette, Felix."

Felix nodded, "Aye, her," he said. "well, anywey, ye should see the tourists they get just because o' that...millions o' them...millions!"

Erchie looked up from his glass.

"Ye don't expect the Holy Mither tae come *HERE*, dae ye?" he sniped. "She'd never find the bloody place for a start!"

All agreed that their small island was just too far out of the way and had nothing to offer.

Felix offered to do a fixed amount of praying to the Blessed Virgin...asking her to pay them a visit and get them out of their jam. They scoffed at the suggestion and the meeting broke up with heavy heart and with not one single idea between them...only Felix's crackpot offer.

But the old man was determined to make restitution and, over the next few weeks, Felix could be seen climbing up to the ruins and crashing down on his knees and fervently bombarding heaven with his petition.

It was Friday night again and the Parish Council was in full swing. The idea of 'Buy-a-Brick' had been mooted by Father

McGinty but had been quickly dismissed as "Hauf o' them couldnae even gie ye chinge of hauf-a-brick" by Erchie Campbell.

Wullie Thomson was at his usual stance by the window sipping his pint. Father McGinty and the rest were at the table bemoaning the fact that a door-to-door collection had raised the paltry sum of Eighteen pounds, twenty-seven pence and a French franc.

"Wi' nae church, we'll jist have tae become atheists," Erchie bemoaned. They turned quickly as they heard Wullie splutter on his drink and give out a piercing cry.

"Good God!" Wullie hollered, wiping his chin with his cuff, 'C'mere...look at this!"

The group hurried over to the window and their jaws dropped.

Felix Urquhart was racing crazily down the hill as though being chased by an invisible foe. His arms were waving frantically and he kept looking round as he weaved and staggered downwards...obviously greatly agitated.

He crashed through the pub door, and slammed it shut, sliding down and pressing his back against the heavy mahogany.

Father McGinty took hold of the breathless Felix and pulled him to his feet...putting an arm around him and steering him towards a chair at the table. McDougall filled a glass of whisky right to the brim and held it to the old man's mouth. Felix steadied McDougall's hand and downed the lot in one go. McDougall replenished the glass and Felix managed to take it from him without spilling a drop. That, too, vanished down his gullet in one quick gulp.

Felix took a deep breath:

"Ah...Ahh...saw him!" he gasped.

The men looked at each other, puzzled.

"Eh?" Erchie said, knitting his brows.

"Ah saw him...as plain as Ah'm seein' you right noo," Felix stammered, holding up his glass for a re-fill, which McDougall quickly did so that nothing would hold Felix back from his mysterious narrative.

"Say that again..." Wullie said.

"Ah saw him...an' he spoke tae me."

"Ye mean ye saw *HER*, Felix...*HER*," Father McGinty said, his voice trembling. Felix vigorously shook his head.

"Naw...*HIM*," he stammered, "definitely *HIM!*"

"Who is *HIM*?" Wullie wanted to know.

Felix held up his glass and McDougall had no hesitation in filling it up...anything to get the wee man on with his tale.

"Well," Felix began, after gulping down the nectar, "Ah was jist finishin' ma prayers when all of a sudden there was a great flash o' lightnin'...and suddenly there he was...hoverin'."

"Ah think ye're bloody haverin'!" Erchie snapped.

Felix ignored him.

"He was jist hoverin' there...six feet aff the grun' – and starin' at me. Ma whole boady began tae shake an' quiver..."

"Ye're boady's like that a' the bloody time," Erchie sniped.

Father McGinty glowered at Erchie and gave Felix a prod.

"Go on, Felix," he urged. "Go on."

"Well," Felix continued, enjoying the attention, "he jist hovered there and stared at me. Ah got the fright o' ma life." He held up his glass and McDougall grumbled under his breath and quickly poured triples out all round. The men strained forward, not wanting to miss a single word.

"Right, whit happened?" Wullie said impatiently.

"Well," Felix went on, "Ah nodded tae him an' he nodded tae me. Who are you, Ah asked nonchal...er...nonchall...Ah said?"

The men shuffled closer.

"Who dae ye think Ah am?" he said.

"How should Ah know, Ah said? Well, ye *SHOULD* know, he said. Well, Ah've never seen you in ma life before, Ah said...or Ah would have definitely remembered. Ah said. Then he telt me who he was..."

Felix fell silent and the men, frustrated at his coyness stood up, feeling they would like to strangle him.

"Well, who the hell was it?" Erchie bawled, clenching his fists.

Felix took his time in answering.

"It was BIG MICK himsel'," he said finally..."Saint Michael...IN PERSON!"

There was a stunned silence. Then gasps of incredulity. It was Wullie Campbell who finally broke the silence.

"Did he say why *SHE* couldnae come hersel'" he said, furrowing his eyebrows.

"He didnae mention her at a'," Felix said, "but he was definitely no' pleased aboot the church bein' burnt doon," Felix said.

"Well, that's straight enough!" Father McGinty exclaimed. "Did he say anythin' else?"

Felix nodded. "Aye, he said Ah've tae go up tae the church every Friday night as usual at hauf-past-seven an' say ma prayers for ma maw as Ah always dae...an' that he wants the church built again as soon as possible."

"Er...whit did Big Mi...er...St Michael look like?" Father McGinty inquired intrestedly.

Felix stroked his chin: "Well," he began slowly, "he was a big fella...aboot six-feet-two an' had blond hair an' a big white goon...right doon tae his feet...an...er...there was somethin' else strikin' aboot him...whit wis it, noo...?" Felix pondered.

Father McGinty drummed his fingers impatiently on the table-top "Think, Felix...think!!"

Felix snapped his fingers. "Ah remember noo," he cried in triumph... "it was a big pair o' purple wings..."

Exasperated, the men looked at each other.

"Purple wings?" Erchie scoffed, throwing his eyes up towards the ceiling.

"Aye, BIG purple wings," Felix reiterated.

Erchie threw up his arms in despair.

"Ah've never heard such baloney in ma entire life," he cried. "PURPLE WINGS...it's a bloody big burd ye've seen!"

"BIG BURDS DON'T TALK!" Felix snapped.

"Big parrots dae," Erchie said smugly.

They talked of nothing else that night. Nobody could believe such a wild story and, after Felix had left, Father McGinty reluctantly had to agree that Felix, after the talk of Lourdes, had connected the yarn...but for the genuine reasons.

The word soon got around about Felix's alleged encounter with St Michael and, on Friday, a small gathering of the older women accompanied him up the hill to the ruined church and saw, as soon as he arrived, he would crash down on his knees and his mouth would move as though he were talking to some invisible being. They heard nothing and they saw nothing. But, to the more devout, this was not unusual.

Old Lizzie McGeachie *DID* swear that she saw a whole gathering of the heavenly host in a corner of the church with

Gabriel blowing his trumpet and the rest dancing to the swinging tune of 'Oh, When the Saints Go Marching In'. But she was quickly despatched to her bed.

Felix turned to the crowd:

"Ah have been told by the Mighty St Michael," he said. "that we wull see oor church rise again frae the ashes...just like the Phamie...on condition that nae mair plates are took and that we ur mair careful when lightin' matches. He has telt me that ma maw is daein' fine and, through his good, ausp...er...help, Ah wull see her soon...although he didnae say whether Ah was tae go doon there or she was comin' up here. Ah hiv been ordered by the Big Yin tae be here next Friday as per usual..." Felix stuck out his chest but had to brave a few cat calls as he clambered down the hill.

The crowd dispersed, muttering and wondering. Father McGinty had taken Felix aside.

"Are you tellin' the truth, Felix...aboot your meetin' wi'...well, you know who. Or are ye just tryin' tae create a diversion...tae take the heat aff yersel'...know whit Ah mean?"

"Ah swear, Father, that Ah see him, so Ah dae, so Ah dae!" Felix was hurt.

The scene at the church was repeated the following Friday with Felix on his knees and seen silently talking to his alleged heavenly visitor. Afterwards he had turned to the crowd and, puffing out his chest, said:

"Ma Big Pal has telt me that everythin' is goin' tae plan...and that Jeannie McPherson is gonny have twins...two lassies..."

There were a few giggles from the younger ones in the crowd, others laughed their heads off and Felix had to shake off Auld Lizzie McGeachie, who was down on her knees and hanging on to his turnups.

Such events could not be hidden from the outside world. Word soon got out about the apparitions at St Michael's Isle...and the newspapermen and television crews began to arrive in their hordes.

The Scottish Tourist Board did a Highland Fling with joy and the faithful flocked in in their thousands.

The locals packed in as many visitors as they could and marquees sprung up all over the island.

The twice-monthly ferry was now twice-daily. Larger boats were put into service to accommodate the caravanners. All of Scotland's airports were working flat out to cater for the huge influx from all corners of the globe.

But many still believed that Felix was still lying...and nobody more so than the Bishop. The police, too, were sniffing about...on the look-out for fraud.

Finally the Bishop decided that the time had come to accost Felix and have the matter settled once and for all. It was difficult for the old man to escape the island without being noticed...for Felix was the 'star' and was hounded and sought out by the hungry faithful and sniffing journalists.

With Father McGinty at his side Felix boarded the ferry in heavy disguise...wearing a false ginger beard and hobbling on crutches. The crutches were not out of place as the entire island seemed to be limping.

After the boat trip and a two-hour train journey, the two men found themselves being ushered into a well carpeted room where a roaring fire crackled in a low grate and the bishop sat majestically behind a huge oak desk. He rose when Father McGinty and Felix entered and greeted them warmly, indicating that they would be seated.

"Well, now," the bishop began, putting his hands together steeple fashion, "I know, Felix, that you are an honourable man and that you have nothing but good, sincere intentions..."

Father McGinty nodded approvingly.

"But," the bishop went on, a frown crossing his face, "can you honestly tell me that the great St Michael, the Archangel, *REALLY* appears and talks to you?"

Felix nodded.

"He does, Your Honour!" Felix replied, putting his hand on his heart.

"He actually speaks to you...tells you things?" the bishop said in disbelief.

"He does, Your Gracefulness" Felix replied proudly. "He even telt me that Wee Jeannie McPherson is gonny have twins."

"Were you surprised at that, Felix? That this great warrior of heaven should talk such...mundane things?"

"Not only was Ah surprised, Your Majesty, but so was Wee

Jeannie McPherson."

"Tell me, Felix, what does St Michael look like?"

Felix sighed. He was fed up answering this question and thought that the message should have been driven home by this time.

"He's a big fella," he said, parrot fashion, "wi' blond hair, a white goon...and big enormous purple wings..."

The bishop sighed and flopped back on his chair. Then, straightening up, he leaned forward.

"Tell me, Felix," he said, drawing his heavy brows together, "Can you, in all sincerity assure me that you haven't been put up to all this? That there's no-one who has cajoled you into this...to help raise cash for the new church, for instance?"

Father McGinty jumped up to protest but was silenced by a gesture from the anxious bishop.

"Ah know whit ye're thinking', Your Omnipotentum," Felix said, sighing deeply, "but you are wrang! The Big Fella *DOES* visit me...and it's no' a Marks an' Spencer publicity stunt either! Him an' me are good pals noo. In fact he is arrangin' a meetin' between me an' ma dear auld deid maw, so he is!"

The interrogation went on for some time before the Bishop finally dismissed them. He was not at all convinced of Felix's sincerity and wondered if the old man was just trying to make up for his folly?

Father McGinty and Felix headed back home but not before a few stops to refresh themselves.

The Bishop lay down that night and worried ·about Felix's answers. He decided to send one of his aides over to the island...in time for the next 'visitation'.

As they stepped off the packed ferry Father McGinty was delighted to see that there had been no let-up in the tourist invasion during their brief sojourn to the mainland. And he was more delighted when he saw that the parish coffers were spilling over.

The Parish Council convened as usual and there was a loud cheer when it was announced that the target for the new church had been reached...and had, in fact, been passed. The Americans, as usual, were more than generous as they always are in such circumstances, Father McGinty said.

Only one Transatlantic visitor had halved his donation when Father McGinty had refused to re-title the church St Michael of the Alamo.

That same night it was also announced that Wee Jeannie McPherson was in labour and McDougall immediately set up a round as a pre-wetting of the baby's head celebration.

The following Friday was suddenly upon them and Felix began his trek up the hillside for his encounter with St Michael and, he hoped, his mother, too!

Wullie Thomson, at McDougall's window as usual, watched the crowd follow Felix up the hill and head for the ruined church.

"Is this no' the night that Felix is tae meet his auld maw?" Wullie asked, turning towards the group at the table. Nobody knew for sure, although Father McGinty said he thought that Felix *had* mentioned something of the sort during their visit to the mainland.

The tall, thin Bishop's aide had now joined them and was looked on with mistrust by the locals. If anyone was going to slam their Felix, it would be them...and they alone!

McDougall's was doing a roaring trade now and a raucous sing-song was going full blast. It was the sound of Father McGinty's fist crashing down on the table that brought a sudden silence to the pub.

"In all due respect tae Big M...er...St Michael," Father McGinty said, "Ah think we should now all make oor way up tae the church..."

A murmer went round the customers and slowly and quietly they left the bar, crossed the street and walked up the steep hill.

Felix was nowhere to be seen...as was St Michael and the crowd were becoming a little hostile. A chant went up demanding that Felix should appear and dissenting voices became louder...calling the whole thing a fraud and confidence trick. Father McGinty began to get worried and ran a finger under his wet, clerical collar. It was the tall, hawkish Bishop's Aide who stepped in and held up his hands like the old time evangelist.

"My friends," he cried, "go back to your home. You have been duped by a little man – a drunk who could not face the consequences of a drunken escapade when he razed your beautiful church to the ground, or WAS it an accident...or...or a

Satanic assault? Shall we ever know?"

Father McGinty began to protest but the grumbling crowd were already dispersing and heading down the hill...some angrily threatening Felix...if they ever caught up with him.

"Home, home with you," the Aide called after them. "There have been no apparitions here...you have been fooled. The church never DID give approbation to this...this farce..."

He stepped down and approached Father McGinty.

"I'm surprised at you, Father, to have allowed yourself to be taken in by this...this person! I will be giving a full report about this fiasco to His Grace the Archbishop. Good day, Father!"

Father McGinty watched the Aide vanish in the crowd as he made his way down the hill. He sadly shook his head.

"Come on," he said, turning to Wullie Thomson and Erchie Campbell, "Let's see if we can find Felix!"

The men made their way down the hill...followed by some of the angry crowd. The obvious place to start their search was Felix's little cottage at the far end of the island. They made their way over the rough terrain, many picking up sticks and stones as they went. The yellow light from the old man's oil-lamp could be seen as they approached the house. Smoke billowed from the chimney top.

Father McGinty was first to arrive at the cracked door. He knocked just once and didn't wait for a reply. Pulling down the rusty, iron latch he marched straight inside...with some of the mob in his wake.

Felix was sitting at his table, a wide smile on his almost toothless face...and he was dead! Father McGinty made a quick sign of the cross and felt the old man's pulse.

"He's gone," he said sadly.

"An easy wey oot o' it!" somebody called and a brick shattered the cottage window. Father McGinty called for order and pleaded with the crowd to have some respect for the dead.

He turned towards Felix and noticed a note in front of him and, still clutched in his hand, an old fashioned quill pen. Father McGinty took up the note and there was a sudden hush from the crowd as he began to read:

"Big Mick came as promised...an' he brought ma auld maw wi' him...but she was beautiful an' young...an' jist as Ah remember her when Ah was a wee boy. An' the Big Fella says that he has been authorised by a higher authority for to let me stey wi' ma mammy. So, we're going hame noo...so cheerio...oh, and by the way, he's right happy that ye've got enough tae restore the church..."

There was a long, reverent silence which was only shattered by the excited cry from Doctor Hamish McLaren, who dashed up yelling..."It's Wee Jeannie...she's had twins...two lovely wee lassies!"

There was a roar of approval from the crowd and everyone laughed. They would leave Felix alone, in peace and go back up the hill and give thanks. They laid the old man down on the bed and quietly closed the door.

Father McGinty turned back to be alone with his old parishioner for a moment of solitude. Looking down on the happy face of Felix, he smiled.

"Thanks, Felix," he murmured, "and God Bless ye'...aye, God Bless ye..."

He turned to leave but stopped and, bending down, took the quill from Felix's hand.

It had been fashioned from a large feather...a large *PURPLE* feather!

Santa Joe

Old Joe rubbed the condensation from his window with his mittened hand...He peered out into the street and shivered as he saw the heavy snow falling.

His tired eyes caught the magic twinkling of the fairy lights from the frosted windows down the row of tenements. His eyes followed them all the way down the street...the yellows and greens and blues...a rainbow strip dancing joyously. He turned away from the window and hobbled over to the dying embers glowing weakly in the grate. Taking a long, iron poker, as though it were a magic wand, he began to prod the pale ash hoping to inject some new life into it. Joe flopped down on to the tattered moquette armchair, lit his pipe and leaned back, watching the blue smoke rising towards the peeling ceiling.

His eyes swept around the room. It was dull and dreary...lifeless! It was different when Mary was here. Then it was sparkling and glowed with life. But when Mary went, the life went out of the house...and out of Joe, too.

Joe and Mary never had children and had decided that it had been the Good Lord's plan. Adoption was out of the question because of Mary's poor health! She always said that Joe would have made a wonderful dad! Joe smiled. Yes! Yes!

Just one week to go and it would be Christmas Day!

For Joe it would be just another day. He had never been much of a religious man, although Mary used to spruce herself up on a Sunday and attend the service at the big church around the corner. She would watch over him after she was gone, she would say – put in a good word for him with the Almighty. An 'almighty' rash statement, Joe reckoned with a wry smile!

Joe pulled himself up from the chair and shuffled over to the coal bunker. There might just be enough dross at the bottom to keep the ailing fire alive! His shovel hit the bare boards. He sighed and decided to investigate his larder. There were some tins there...mostly of baked beans...but one can had the added attraction of containing mini-pork sausages also...with tomato ketchup. He would keep that for his Christmas Day treat, he decided.

He opened a can of beans, heated them on the gas ring on the hob and tucked in. Beans were good for you, he thought. Sure, weren't the cowboys in the pictures brought up on them? Joe chuckled!

Joe washed the plate, leaving it to drip-dry at the side of the sink. He took a towel and studied his face on the cracked wall mirror above the grate. His flowing white beard and moustache were stained red with the ketchup. He wiped them clean, gave his beard a fluff-up and stood back and surveyed his countenance. Yes, he was a fine figure of a man, he decided!

He didn't get out much these days because of a slight heart condition...but nothing serious! Maybe Mary *WAS* looking after him, true enough.

He managed to get down for his pension, on Thursdays and have a quiet stroll about the streets before returning home. The children in the street dubbed him Santa...and Old Joe was pleased with the tag. Another myth...SANTA! Still, children need myths, Joe thought...and, perhaps, adults did, too!

Aye, if only Mary and he had had children! They'd be grown up by now...but there would be grandchildren to sit on his knee. They would laugh and dream of what Santa might bring...

"Will you leave something at the fireplace for Santa when he comes, grandad?" they would say. Sure, he would! How about half-a-tin of baked beans...in tomato sauce, eh? And they would giggle and give him a hug before piling into their dad's red car and speeding off home to their very own Christmas tree...and their own, special gift for Santa Claus. And if they asked him what *HE* wanted for Christmas he would tell them, "You...just you!"

Joe puffed at his pipe and laughed at his crazy thoughts. Perhaps he *would* leave something for a weary Santa...half-a-tin of baked beans, eh? If the old boy with the red suit and barrelled tummy didn't show up, the timerous wee mouse who's been visiting him would soon make short work of it.

He would think about it! He hadn't seen his little friend, the mouse, for a while. He hoped it hadn't fallen foul of a marauding cat! Or maybe he had moved on to a house with better company! Who could blame him?

Joe did not hear the quiet knock on the door at first. Then it became louder and more persistent. Who could this be, Joe wondered? he *NEVER* got visitors...Nobody *EVER* rapped on his door. Joe shuffled over and slowly opened the door. A small, chubby man clutching a brown paper parcel and wearing a clerical collar stood there.

"Mr McKenzie?" the man asked.

"Aye, that's me," Joe said, wondering why a clergyman would be visiting HIM?

The little man smiled broadly.

"I'm Mr Stewart...that's my church round the corner."

"Ah never go there!" Joe snapped.

"Oh, I know that," Mr Stewart said, "but I believe your dear departed wife did at one time?"

Joe nodded. "Aye, but that was a long time ago," he said quietly. The minister gave a slight cough.

"Ye...yes...aye...I know," he stammered. "I was wondering if I could have a few words with you, Mr McKenzie?"

Joe's eyes went to the brown paper parcel the minister was holding. Could be a food parcel, he thought, his eyes lighting up.

"Aye, come away in," he said, opening his door wider. The minister stepped into the sparsely furnished room. He let his eyes sweep over the place and could see the poverty and feel the loneliness.

"Sit ye doon, meenister," Joe said, indicating his favourite moquette chair. The minister sank into the chair which was 'way past its best and could do with being re-sprung. He put the parcel down on the floor by his side.

"Would ye like a wee cuppa tea, Meenister?" Joe asked, heading for the kettle on top of the sink. The minister, in his worldly wisdom, nodded. He knew that many barriers crumbled over a good cup of tea. Joe smiled!

"That's very good of you, Mr McKenzie," Mr Stewart said, "There's nothing to beat a hot cup of tea on a cold night, eh?"

"Aye, and it's better if you've got a wee dram tae put in it, eh?" Joe winked and the minister laughed. The two men were soon sipping sweet, hot tea and chatted about the world in general and nothing in particular. Joe was glad of the company!

It had been a long time since a stranger sat in the chair! Not like the old days when he arrived home from the shipyards, dirty and greasy, with Mary waiting there with a hot dinner. They had visitors then, too. Yes, visitors!

The wee minister was not a bit stuffy. Joe thought. Quite pleasant, in fact and seemed to know what was going on in the world! Joe's eyes kept going to the brown paper parcel. The minister hadn't given a reason for his visit and Joe began to shift uneasily in his chair. Finally, Mr Stewart put his cards on the table.

"Mr McKenzie," he began, "next Saturday is Christmas Day and we, in the church, have been collecting donations to give deprived children a Christmas party in the church hall...and, by heaven, there's plenty of them, Mr McKenzie...an awful lot!"

Joe knitted his brows.

"Aw, Ah'm awfu' sorry, minister. Ah really like weans," he said, "but Ah've only got ma pension...but maybe Ah could gie ye sixpence or..."

Mr Stewart vigorously shook his head:

"No, no!" he exclaimed. "You don't understand. I wouldn't expect you to..."

He didn't get finishing. Joe put up his hand.

"Ah've got ma presentation watch, right enough," Joe said, "Maybe Ah could pawn it...Ah got it when Ah left the yerds – forty-two years service," he said proudly...

"No, no, not at all, Mr McKenzie," the minister said quickly, "It's not that! We've received more than enough to give the kiddies a good time and a wee present...what we need is a Santa Claus!"

Santa Claus? Me Santa Claus!" Old Joe shook his head: "Naw, naw, ye've got the wrang man, Reverend," he said flatly. "Ah couldnae swindle the weans...Ah widdnae feel right. Ye canny dae somethin' ye don't believe in."

The minister understood. Old men like Joe had their principles. He would try again.

"Look Mr McKenzie," he said softly, "who's to say that there's no Santa Claus, no good fairies or wicked fairies, witches and goblins, elves and angels? Who's to say?"

"Ach, ye don't believe in a' that rubbish, meenister, dae ye?" Joe chuckled.

"There are more things in heaven and earth than meets the eye," Mr Stewart replied, quoting the Good Book.

Joe shook his head:

"Ah suppose," he said, "that it's your joab tae believe in angels and miracles an' a' that. But no' Santa, surely no' Santa?"

Mr Stewart sighed.

"Those children believe in him," he said. "To them he's as real as you and me. They know about him, have read about him although, God knows, he's never visited most of them. YOU may not be the real thing but you're what they've got and to them you ARE that big, jolly, tubby miracle man...the man of dreams. And who's to say that YOU are not Santa Claus? If they *BELIEVE* in you, then you *ARE* he."

Old Joe stroked his beard. Maybe the good reverend was right! To the world, he was just a lonely old man with a few tins of baked beans in a cupboard. There was no opportunity for him to bring Christmas joy to anybody! Maybe, just maybe, for once...he was WANTED...he was NEEDED! He walked over to the window and gazed out. The lights still flashed behind those frosted windows. Each one of those homes had a Santa Claus, a DAD, a Father...a FATHER CHRISTMAS. He turned.

"A'right, meenister," he said, Ah'll dae it...just for the sake o' the weans...an' whit you said."

Mr Stewart beamed! He began unwrapping the paper parcel. Joe watched eagerly. He felt a bit disappointed when Mr Stewart pulled out a bright red, woollen Santa Claus costume.

"There's one thing we won't need...and that's a beard," the minister laughed.

"They never get the beards right anyway," Joe said, proudly stroking his own set of fine whiskers. "Like dods o' cotton wool, so they are!" he added.

The costume boots shone like ebony and the broad belt had a shining, golden buckle.

"The buckle is usually silver," the minister said, "but we managed to get this golden one...after all gold *WAS* one of the gifts placed at the manger on that first Christmas Day, eh?"

Joe shrugged:

"Aye, well if ye believe in a' that," he muttered. Mr Stewart rose and shook the old man's hand:

"You'll never regret this!" he said. "You'll be rewarded in other ways." He slipped a five pound note into Joe's hand. Joe stared at the money. He could do a lot with that cash but, shaking his head, he thrust it back into the minister's hand.

"Naw, naw," he said adamantly, "this is MA present for the weans. It's no' a present if ye're gettin' peyed for it, is it? And besides," he went on, his voice dropping, "Ah've got naebody else tae gie a present tae."

Mr Stewart suddenly felt humbled! No use protesting. Joe was a man of principles. He put the note back into his wallet.

"Aye, well...er...we'll see you at the church hall about twelve o'clock Saturday, then eh?" he said.

Joe nodded:

"On the button," he said. Joe opened the door and Mr Stewart shook his hand warmly before descending the steep stairs and stepping into the cold chill of night. He had learned a lot! Turning up his coat collar he headed down the road, round the corner and on towards the church...with the happy news that he had found a Santa.

Joe had found an old coat hanger at the bottom of the sideboard and had lovingly placed the costume on it and hanged it up on the clothes pulley. Over the next few nights he would just sit and gaze at the red woollen costume. Secretly, he couldn't wait for the 'Big Day' to arrive so that he could put it on. He would stand in front of the mirror, with just the pom-pom hat on and practice his 'HO-HO-HO' dialogue until he was satisfied that he'd got it just right.

He took great pride in polishing and repolishing the gleaming black leather boots and buffing up the gold-plated belt. He would shampoo his whiskers until they were snow white. He wouldn't let the good Reverend Stewart or, more importantly, 'the weans' down. Suddenly the idea of becoming a Santa Claus, even just for a day, filled his whole being! For the first time in many years he would not be alone on Christmas Day. Maybe Mary had arranged it, he thought with a smile. She knew how he loved children. Yes, he *WOULD* be Father Christmas...he *WAS* Father Christmas!

The week seemed to drag on until suddenly it was Christmas Eve. Joe began his preparations early that evening. He gave his whiskers their final treatment until they resembled pure, white cotton wool. He stood back from the mirror..."Perfect!", he decided. He checked the suit, making sure that every wrinkle had vanished. He had pressed it and re-pressed it with the old iron. Now, it had fully passed muster. He placed it back on to the pulley.

Old Joe found it hard to sleep that night. His eyes kept going to the costume, swaying up there on the pulley in the middle of the kitchen like a crimson spectre floating near the ceiling! Tomorrow would be his happiest day for years.

Joe awoke to find sunlight streaming in the window. He glanced at his bedside alarm clock...ten a.m. Time to move!

The sound of happy laughter drew him to the window. Outside, in the snow-covered street, he saw cowboys and spacemen shooting at each other. Little girls had become loving, affectionate mothers as they proudly pushed prams with plastic babies tucked up inside...leaning over now and again and making sure that baby was sleeping soundly. Snowballs became missiles and Joe smiled and nodded. Santa had been busy during the night!

He took the costume down from the clothes pulley and placed it in a battered old suitcase. He would sneak into one of the ante-rooms in the hall, unobserved and then he would, on a signal, make his grand entrance. He practiced his 'HO-HO-HO' once more and was entirely satisfied! He sat down and lit up his pipe. Mary would be proud of him, he thought. Joe glanced at the clock...11 a.m. Time to go! He picked up the suitcase and headed for the door. Hesitating, he turned, walked to the cupboard and retrieved a half-can of baked beans...with mini-pork sausages...and placed it by the fireplace. He smiled; "Just in case ye're workin' overtime," he laughed, peering up the chimney.

Joe turned to leave. He was excited. The pain came suddenly...like a vice crushing his chest. His head began to swim and his legs buckled and everything went black. Old Joe sagged to the floor. Outside, the children yelled and played. Inside the house, Joe lay crumpled on the floor his hand grasping an old suitcase.

Joe's eyes flickered open. Slowly, as he focussed, he looked round the room. Darkness had come down and the street was quiet. The pain had gone now. Joe, very carefully, pulled himself up on to his feet. He stumbled over to the light switch and switched on. He glanced at the clock by his bedside...7.30 p.m. Suddenly the fog enveloping his mind cleared. He stared down at the suitcase. The Children? He sighed and flopped down on to the armchair. He had let everyone down...Mr Stewart, the children...everybody! Even this one moment of happiness had been denied him, he thought! Mary had got it all wrong. The Reverend Stewart had got it all wrong!

A sudden rapping at the door shook him. Slowly, he shuffled over and opened the door widely. The Reverend Stewart stood in the shadow.

"Mr McKenzie," he said, "are you all right?" Joe beckoned the minister to enter.

"Look Mr Stewart," Joe said quietly, "Ah'm really sorry. Ah must've had a wee blackout...Ah get them sometimes, it's the auld ticker, y'see! They're no' serious and Ah've got pills frae the doactor for them. Ah suppose Ah must've forgot tae take them this moarnin'...wi' a' the excitement an' that, know whit Ah mean?"

Joe indicated a chair and Mr Stewart sat down.

"What *DO* you mean?" he asked. Joe shuffled his feet.

"Were the weans disappointed?" he asked quietly. "Did ye have time tae get somebody else?"

Mr Stewart furrowed his brows. "What *ARE* you talkin' about, Mr McKenzie? YOU were the best Santa Claus we've ever had. You had the children singing and clapping and jumping for joy. It was YOU that made their day! We'll have you every year from now on."

Old Joe tried to grasp what the minister was saying. "Bu...But..." he started. Mr Stewart held up his hand:

"I really came round to thank you again, Mr McKenzie and remind you that our own Christmas dinner is at half-past-eight. You WILL be there, now, won't you? Round at the manse, Mrs Stewart will shoot me if you're not."

Joe was speechless and Mr Stewart burst out laughing.

"This fell off your costume," he said, holding up a gold-plated buckle. "It's a wonder your trousers didn't fall down, eh?" Mr Stewart slapped Joe in the back and chortled gleefully.

Joe stared at the gleaming buckle and hurried over to the suitcase. Flinging the lid open, he pulled out the neatly packed costume.

His jaw dropped open! The gold-plated buckle was missing. Mr Stewart replaced the buckle, bent down and closed the case.

"I was going to take this costume back with me...but you'd be as well keeping it here. You'll be needing it again, eh?" The minister turned at the door: "See you later then Mr McKen...er...Joe, and thanks again." The minister could be heard whistling as he went down the stairs.

Joe flopped on the chair. His mind was racing! Who had taken his place? He stood up, walked over to the window and gazed up at the nightly sky. It was a black, star studded velvet sky with a pale moon throwing shadows. The stars twinkled and flashed like jewels and seemed to be within easy clutching distance. A shooting star suddenly streaked across the sky leaving a silver stream in its wake. Joe rubbed his eyes. For a moment he thought he saw somebody waving down at him. His eyes were playing tricks on him! He turned and went back to his chair. He reckoned that one of the parishioners, noting that he hadn't shown up, and not wanting to disappoint the children, had taken his place without letting on to anybody. Yes, that was the answer, Joe decided. Joe sat down again at his chair by the fireside. He lit up his pipe and, after a while, his eyes fell on the tin of beans down at the fireside. Joe bent over and peered inside. The can was half-empty!

Then his eye caught the little mouse scurrying to safety behind the fireplace. Joe smiled, the culprit had been spotted. There's always an explanation, Joe thought to himself. So, the wee mouse hadn't changed his digs after all? Joe was glad.

Joe checked the time on the mantleshelf clock. Time he was making tracks for the manse and his new friends. He opened up the suitcase for one, last look at the costume before putting it away until next year.

He took it out and held it up at arms length. Yes, he was made for it, no doubt about it, he decided.

He tenderly folded it, placed it back in the battered case and softly closed the lid.

He hadn't noticed the red stains on the collar...bright red...just like tomato ketchup!

A Christmas Ball

Alex Rodgers had volunteered for the Christmas duty. Well, it was expected of him! He was the only one with no family – no ties. The crew had already left the observatory, hurrying home to warm firesides, Christmas trees, paper hats and roasted turkeys...and families.

Family life had escaped Alex, he had no-one. There was nobody to build a snowman for, to light up the tree for or a rosy-face to watch as a present was opened to a scream of delight. He DID get pangs of envy sometimes when he heard the lads at the Observatory talk of their children and girlfriends and wives.

He was an orphan and nobody cared a damn if he was stuck halfway up this mountain or floating face down in a rough sea. Probably nobody even knew he was up here keeping his eye on the heavens. No aunts, no uncles, no brothers or sisters or cousins, no anybody. It looked to Alex that that was how it was planned by whoever it was 'up there'.

It was Christmas Eve and he sat alone inside the warm observation room. He let his eyes wander around the walls...all decked with Christmas cards and greetings...to Wullie...to Sammy...Angus...none to Alex!

Alex shook himself out of his self pity and switched on the radio. A church choir sang the old, traditional carols and Alex, leaning back on his chair with his feet on the desk, whistled an accompaniment.

He checked the screen and noted that all was clear. He got up and switched on the coffee machine and sat back. The screen emitted a monotonous bleep and it never wavered...never changed. The heavens were quiet this Christmas Eve. He stood up and looked out of the window...no snow! The stars pulsated in a silk-black sky. A tawny moon hung like a Chinese lantern and bathed the mountain in a warm glow. The gurgling of the coffee machine made Alex turn. He poured himself a large mugful, took a sip and smacked his lips as the sweet taste slid down his parched throat.

He wondered how the lads were getting on? Big Bill probably had the tree well decorated by now and the presents gift wrapped and lying underneath...ready for the morning onslaught by screaming, jumping happy children. He's probably got a large whisky in his hand by now, Alex reckoned...He wouldn't mind a dram himself...but that was forbidden. Not while on duty...even if it was Christmas. He settled for the coffee, raised his mug to the moon and stars and wished them well. The radio choir sang on – 'Silent Night'. For Alex that's just what it was. He wondered if anybody was out there? Could it be that on a faraway planet somebody, just like him, was sitting on a mountain, gazing out and wondering the same thing? He shrugged..."Poor sucker!" he thought. It got him thinking. Why not? Why should he be alone in this great expanse of Universe? Maybe there WAS some other Alex Rodgers out there, wondering if HE was there? Would it be Christmas there? If the Almighty had made all of the universe then surely there must be other Alexs' on other planets!

Alex topped up his coffee. The steaming brew consoled him and he was comforted by the quiet singing coming from the radio. Alex glanced up at the wall clock – 11.45 p.m. It was time to check the huge radio telescope. Clad in his heavy duty anorak, he pulled the hood up and pushed his hands deeply into his pockets. The night air strung him as he stepped outside into the freezing night. Breathing warmth into his hands, he quickly went round the three large 'scopes and checked them out. Satisfied that all was in order, he stood at the doorway and took in large gulps of clean, cold mountain air.

Down below, in the valley, he could make out the coloured, flashing Christmas lights of the small town. There would be parties going on down there – people, life and gaiety. Excited children would be tucked up for the night with one eye open for the sound of sleigh bells. For wasn't Santa on his way? His eyes swept over the heavens. No sign of a sleigh anywhere! He smiled and stepped back into the welcoming heat of the observatory.

Alex brewed up some more coffee and filled his mug. Checking the screen once more, he lit up a cigarette and sat down at his cluttered desk. The radio choir sang on..."God Rest Ye Merry

Gentlemen…"

Alex wasn't much of a praying man! Long ago he had decided that you come into this world, fight your way through it, and go out again!

In between times nobody gives a damn! You're on your own and, if the breaks come along, you're lucky!

Twelve o'clock struck from the wall clock. Christmas Day! Alex raised his mug, "Here's tae you, kid!" he said in a mock Humphrey Bogart accent, "Merry Christmas!"

The sudden broken rhythmic pulse from the screen made him turn quickly round. There was no doubt about it – the bleeps were going haywire! The screen image was suddenly going crazy…beams zig-zagging all over the monitor. Alex could hardly contain himself. He had never seen anything like this! He quickly checked the connections…everything was okay!

Alex hurried to the window and peered out. His sharp eyes scanned the sky and opened wide in disbelief. His jaw dropped as he grabbed the powerful binoculars. High in the heavens was a golden star…more of a ball. A glistening, gold nugget that shouldn't be there! It was moving slowly towards the east. This was crazy, Alex thought! He looked again. It was there all right, shining and dimming every other celestial body around it. Was it a new star or was it a ship – a spaceship, maybe – an alien ship? The monitor was picking up and tracking this newcomer in the firmament. It was no illusion! Alex was seeing this with his own, incredulous eyes…

Alex flopped down on to his chair and grabbed the phone.

Frantically, he dialled headquarters.

"Get me Simpson," he snapped. The man at the other end was calm…too calm!

"Take it easy!" he said, "Simpson's on holiday, you should know that, Alex!"

"Look Hector, have ye checked yer monitor?" Alex asked breathlessly.

"Aye, haven't we all?" Hector McGeachie replied. "Whit's the problem?"

"Well?" Alex asked anxiously.

"Well whit?" Hector said, a little impatiently.

"Well, can ye no' see the damn thing?" Alex yelled.

"All Ah can see is the moon an' the stars and a lotta nothin' else," Hector said nonchalantly.

"Ye don't see that bloody Golden Star or Ball or whatever the hell it is, travellin' East?"

"Look Alex," Hector said, "Ah know it's Christmas an' all that...but have you been drinkin'?"

"Don't be so stupit!" Alex snapped. "Look again!"

There was a pause and then Hector came back on the line...irritatingly calm.

"There's nuthin' but nuthin' oot there," Hector rasped, "no even Santy Claus goin' across the sky in his sleigh...nae three wise men. It must be that high altitude, Alex, that's gettin' tae ye!"

The phone went dead. Alex slammed his receiver down and hurried back to the window. The golden star, or whatever it was, had stopped and was suspended in space. Alex couldn't understand why Hector couldn't see it in his monitor. It was there for all to see. Or was it? Maybe this isolation WAS getting to him. Perhaps he was seeing this thing only in his mind's eye. Loneliness can play tricks on the imagination!

Alex hoped he wouldn't start talking to himself! That would be a sure sign he was going nuts! The monitor's crazy bleeping suddenly stopped. A pattern began to emerge...a strong, steady pulse. Then it changed again...an intermittent signal. It kept repeating itself over and over again. Alex listened intently. This was a message coming through...a coded communication! Alex tracked the signal and became excited. There was no doubt in his mind – the message was from that thing out there. He grabbed the phone once more.

"Aye?" Hector's voice growled.

"Look, Hector, that golden thing is still up there. Check yer monitor again, will ye?"

"Alex, are ye still oan that jungle juice?" Hector sniped. "There's nuthin' there, Ah'm tellin ye...NUTHIN'!" Alex felt his blood pressure rise.

"Look again, will ye?"

There was a brief silence and an angry voice came back to him.

"Look, Alex," Hector growled, "since you called that last time, Ah've checked it oot wi' the Air Force, the Weather Bureau and the airport. Naebody's got anythin' on their radar...everybody's got NUTHIN', Alex...only you! Noo, take ma advice and close yer eyes for ten minutes and then look again...a'right?"

Alex fell silent. Everybody couldn't be wrong! But what about that coded signal?

"Hector," Alex said, quietly, "Ah'm gettin' a signal...a message."

"Aye, Ah wish ye would get the message, Alex," Hector replied with a sigh.

"Maybe somebody up there disnae like me, eh?" Alex said.

"If ye don't get aff the phone there'll be somebody doon here that disnae like ye, Alex!"

They both laughed and the line went dead. Alex went back to his desk and stared out of the window.

The golden ball was still there. It had hardly moved! He checked the screen. The signal was repeating itself. Alex jotted the signals down on his pad.

There was a definite pattern! He took out the code book from his desk drawer. Meticulously, he pored over the code...the numbers and symbols. When he felt he had it correct, he fed the data into the computer and watched the screen with anticipation. His mouth gaped as the message slowly began to take shape on the green monitor screen..."Merry Christmas Alex Rodgers", it said.

Alex stood gaping at the screen...stunned for a moment. Who or what was the thing out there? There was an intelligence behind it, that was for sure. Someone out there felt HIS loneliness. He suddenly felt a warmth envelope him. Someone out there in that vastness, that eternity CARED.

The shrill ring of the phone startled him.

"Look, Alex," Hector said, "Ah'm sorry if Ah was Bolshy wi' ye earlier on. Are ye a'right?"

"Aye, Ah'm fine," Alex said quietly.

"Ah can understaun' bein' there by yersel, alone, can be pretty boring. Ah should've been mair thoughtful!"

"Who's alone?" Alex said, smiling to himself. He cradled the phone and turning towards his unknown visitor, he raised his mug.

"And a Happy Christmas tae you, tae!" he said, clearing his throat.

Alex cradled the phone, lit a cigarette and leaned back on the chair. The golden ball began to move slowly away. He stood up and watched it drift silently towards the east until it vanished.

He sat down and watched the blue smoke from his cigarette swirl up and vanish, too. It didn't matter who that message had come from. He knew now that he wasn't alone at all. Somebody knew he was here on this planet Earth.

And it was someone...who knew his name!

The Cribbers

Father Brendan Connolly grunted as he rose to his feet, stepped back and smiled with satisfaction... "There!" he said. "What d'ye think?" Old Annie, the church cleaner, switched off the vacuum cleaner and grimaced.

"Aye, it's no' bad, she said. "but have ye no' missed somethin'?"

The old priest's eyes quickly scanned the Christmas crib. "No, I think they're all there, all right," he said, allowing his eyes to go over the figures..."There's Mary and Joseph and the baby in the manger...the shepherds and the animals...that wee goat. Looks fine to me!"

Annie shrugged and switched on the cleaner once more, saying: "Ah just thought there was somethin' missin'!"

It was Christmas Eve and the church would be packed that night for Midnight Mass. In the morning happy children would flock round the crib and the real spirit of Christmas would come to life.

Father Connolly left Annie to her chores and stepped into the cold of the day. He shivered slightly, straightened his biretta and hurried into the rectory which was next door. Snow was falling heavily, quickly leaving a thick, virgin carpet in the town.

Old Tom's foot would start acting up again. The cold did that to his left foot despite the pages of newspaper he wrapped round it. It was during the war, in Tobruk, that a sniper's well-aimed bullet blew off his big toe. From then on, in the winter, it throbbed like a toothache!

Tom had limped around the town most of that day looking for a shelter for the night. It was getting dark now and he found himself outside the park gates. He shuffled through and headed for his favourite bench, in a secluded spot at the far end.

Tom ran the sleeve of his tattered coat over the seat, clearing the two-inches of glistening snow, and slumped down with a heavy sigh. He blew heat into his chilled hands and a sudden, biting blast of wind cut into his chilled body. He cursed that sniper...as he did every winter. His family had perished in the Clydebank blitz and there was nobody now...nobody! He wondered what had happened to his two cronies, Charlie and Archie? He hadn't seen them all day. Maybe they had been lucky, he thought. Perhaps they'd found a good shelter for the night?

Tom pushed the thought from his mind. If the 'Gruesome Twosome', as he called them, *HAD* found a suitable place, they would have searched for him to join them. For they were boyhood pals. They had joined up together when war broke out and had gone through the desert campaign together...old comrades!

"Thought you'd be here!" the voice said. Tom looked up. Charlie and Archie were blowing life into their hands and stamping their weary feet to keep the circulation going.

"Nae luck Ah take it?" Tom said.

Archie shook his head. "Whit dae *you* think?" he sighed, flopping down on the bench beside him.

"There was nae room at the inn!" Charlie said wearily, joining his mates on the bench. The three men sat in silence.

"Y'know!" Tom suddenly said, "Ah'll bet ye that when Mary and Big Joe were huntin' for a place on that first Christmas night, they must've thought that that stable was a godsend! Ah mean, it must've been like gettin' booked intae the Central Hotel, eh?"

Charlie nodded: "Aye, anythin' tae get oot the cauld, Ah'd say!" Archie agreed; "Aye, right enough!" he exclaimed, adding, "Ah widnae mind a wee comfortable stable masel' right noo."

The three men fell into silence once more.

In unison, they each blew heat into their freezing hands. Tom had been thinking and, turning to Archie, said: "Dae ye know any stables, Erchie?" Archie looked up incredulously: "Whit? "Where would ye find a bloomin' stable in Glesca? Ah mean there is nae hoarses nooadays, is there? It's a garage ye need tae look for!"

Charlie looked up: "Ye'd get done for breakin' an' enterin'!" he exclaimed knowingly. Tom nodded in agreement.

"Wan thing," Tom said, "if we found shelter in a garage, we could get well-oiled, eh?" The three men laughed loudly.

"Ah was just thinkin'", Tom went on, "aboot the time when we were in that blazin' desert...and here we are a' freezin' tae death, mind?"

"Who could forget it!" Archie said, a smile flitting across his face. "Mind yon cafe wi that stoatin' dancer wi' a plum in her belly button, eh?"

"Who could forget *HER*?" Charlie laughed.

"She used tae invite us sojers up tae see if we could snatch it wi' oor teeth, remember?" Archie chuckled.

"Aye," Tom said, a faraway look in his eye. "Ah widnae mind bein' wi' her right noo!"

"Ye fancied her, eh?" Charlie said, winking and nudging Tom in the ribs.

"Naw, But Ah fancy that plum!" Tom laughed. Charlie and Archie joined in and then, with a sigh, they fell silent once again.

Charlie finally broke the quietness:

"How's yer foot, Tom?" he inquired.

"If Ah was a hoarse," Tom replied, "they'd shoot me!" The three sat staring into space, each with his own thoughts. Archie, whose wife ran off with his best pal! Charlie, who had looked after his ailing mother until she died and Tom, who lost all that was dear to him.

"Ye'd be deid the noo!" Archie exclaimed, turning to Tom.

Tom's eyebrows shot up: "Eh?"

"If that bullet had got ye in the heid instead o' yer big toe...ye'd be deid the noo," Archie repeated..."If that sniper hadnae've been cock-eyed, ye'd be kickin' up the daises...at least ye're still alive!"

"Ye call this livin'?" Tom scowled.

"Ah don't like daises!" Charlie said.

"Especially when ye're bloody-well lyin' underneath them," Tom cried. There was a pause. Archie had been thinking seriously about life after death.

"Dae ye think they'll learn ye the harp?" he said seriously.

"When ye get up there, Ah mean," Archie said, stabbing his thumb skywards.

"Don't be so daft!" Tom growled, "they've got better things tae dae than teach folk the harp. Ah mean, it would get oan yer bloody nerves sittin' listenin' tae a' that strummin' every day. It widnae be Heaven, then, would it? Ah mean, imagine you an' me meetin' in the heavenly street and you sayin' tae me...'Comin' in for a pint, Tom?' and me sayin', 'Naw, Ah canny, Erchie, Ah'm jist aff tae ma harp lessons', eh?"

Charlie nodded. He couldn't see Tom turning down a pint. "Ye're dead right, Tom," he said, "they're bound tae have pianna players up there as well!"

"Ah don't think they'll have any pubs up there," Archie said.

"It widnae be Heaven, then, would it?" Tom sneered. They've probably got stacks o' pubs…a' sellin' Harp as well."

Charlie licked his lips. It would be pleasant sitting up there, sipping a pint. He thought of his mother and envied her. "Ah'm sure ma maw is up there lookin' efter me," he said.

"Well, she's no' makin' a very good joab o' it, is she?" Archie moaned.

"She's maybe too busy," Tom said, "probably away for her harp lessons a' day!"

The men laughed. Tom stood up and stamped his feet, hoping to push some pain-relieving heat into his tortured, injured foot.

"Ah'll tell ye this," he said, flapping his arms around his body, "Ah don't care if Ah go doon below – at least it'll be warm!"

"Ah wonder if they learn ye the harp doon there?" Archie said, knitting his brows.

"Naw, it'll be the musical saw doon there!" Tom said.

The sound of the Town Hall clock striking midnight made the men look up.

"Well lads, it's Christmas," Tom said, offering his outstretched hand. The men warmly shook each others hand with a chorus of 'Merry Christmas'.

"Sorry Ah've nothin' tae gie youse," Tom said sadly. Charlie dug into his coat pocket.

"Ah've got a fag," he said, "Ah've been keepin' it for this moment!"

Charlie produced a crumpled cigarette packet and pulled out the lone and battered cigarette. Expertly, he broke it into three pieces giving each of his friends a part.

The men took it with gratitude and each lighted up. They, once more, sat down on the damp bench and were quiet. Each cupped his hand around the red, warm glow of the cigarette and, for a moment, they were at peace with the world.

Midnight mass had begun in Father Connolly's church and the three men sat, quietly listening to the carol singing. Little was said as they tuned into the service from the distance. They were sorry when it was all over. They could hear the happy voices of the congregation spilling out into the cold night air. There were cries of 'Happy Christmas' echoing over the rooftops and cheery laughter. And then the roar of engines as all speeded home to families...and warm love.

Tom stood up on the bench and craned his neck over the shrubbery. The lights of the church were out and he could see the last tail-light as the sound of the car's motor became weaker as it vanished in the distance. All was quiet now! No-one spoke, none wanting to break the spell...that momentary warm feeling of spiritual nourishment. Tom snapped his fingers and broke the silence.

"I've got a great idea," he said with enthusiasm, "there's a big empty church up that street...just goin' tae waste!"

"It'll be a' loacked up," Charlie said, screwing up his nose...

"There must be some wey tae get in!" Tom exclaimed. "It'll be warm in there...especially efter a' they folk bein' in there a' night."

Charlie nodded in agreement.

"True enough, Tam," he said, "but we canny just break in...no' tae a chapel, Tam!"

"How no'?" Tom snapped, "It's God's hoose, int it? Besides, if we're caught, Ah canny see the priest turnin' us in...Ah mean, efter a', it *IS* Christmas!"

"It would be a lot warmer, right enough!" Archie said thoughtfully.

"Aye, and we could always eat a couple o' caun'les," Tom said, rubbing his hands, adding, with a twinkle, "A light snack ye might say!" Tom chuckled but Charlie was not so sure. He could see the Almighty's wrath coming down in forked lightning. Things were bad enough, he thought, without them making HIM up there angry.

Tom, as though reading Charlie's thoughts, said quickly: "Ah don't think that HE would be too annoyed. Ah think HE'd turn a blind eye. Efter a', it *IS* his birthday, int it?

Charlie nodded: "Aye, it is," he said, "in which case we would need tae take him a wee present...know whit Ah mean?"

He thrust his hand deep into his pocket and emerged clutching a two-pence piece which he triumphantly held up. "Voila!" he cried.

"Have ye no' got thruppance?" Tom asked hopefully. "That would gie us a penny each tae gie him." Charlie dug deeper but, alas, the bank was empty! Tom decided that they would just have to chance it. They would take their luck in their hands and just hope that the Almighty would be too busy celebrating his son's birthday to notice. The men clambered over the gate and made their way up the street towards the church, now standing empty and quiet. The snow began to fall in large, heavy flakes and they hurried on, desperate to get into the warmth and the shelter. Charlie wondered what candles tasted like? Arriving at the church, the low railing was no problem for the freezing trio. Within seconds they were inside the church grounds and doing a quick reconnoitre. Skirting the building, they found, as expected, every door locked. One small low down window at the rear was their only choice. They argued as to who would do "the dirty deed" and it was finally decided that, as it was Tom who put forward the idea, that it should be he who broke the window pane.

Tom sniffed, threw a glance towards heaven and smashed in the glass with his elbow. All three froze as the glass shattered...but there was no sound of anyone hurrying to the scene.

The welcoming warmth hit the men immediately they stepped into the church. The votive candles still burned brightly and the men stood in the centre aisle in awe as their eyes swept round the magnificent building. There was a silence here that they had never experienced since boyhood days.

"Where will we put the tuppence?" Charlie asked, his voice shaking.

"Gie it tae me," "Tom said thrusting his hand out, "there's bound tae be a boax or somethin'. Charlie, hands trembling, handed over the coin and Tom looked around, his eyes settling on the 'Poor Box' at the bottom of the right hand aisle. Slowly he walked down and deposited the money...not daring to look at the altar.

"That's a' we've got tae give ye," he muttered to his invisible listener. "Sorry aboot that!" Suddenly the story of the widow's mite came into his head. Funny! It had been years since he last heard the story. He wondered why he had suddenly thought of it?

Charlie had been wandering about and was now standing by the crib.

"Look at this!" he whispered, "wee statues...look, a coo and a goat an' that!" He was joined by Archie.

"That's a crib," Archie said knowingly.

"So it is," Tom agreed, "that's Mary and Joseph and...the wee baby Jesus in his wee manger. They blokes staunin' there wi' the big walkin' sticks are shepherds who came doon tae see the wean."

Charlie was amazed at Tom's biblical knowledge. "Ah'll bet they were gled tae get intae that stable and oot o' the cauld weather!" he said.

"It might no' have been cauld," Archie said, "Ah mean they were in the desert, weren't they?"

"Aye, the desert!" Tom said with a faraway look. The men explored the church, taking care not to disturb anything. They held their hands over the candle flames and were cheered by the heat. Wandering about, they ended back at the crib, which was down to the right of the main altar.

"It would've been nice tae have been there, eh?" Tom said, nodding down at the crib.

"Been where?" Charlie asked, furrowing his brow.

"There," Tom said, pointing at the crib, "tae have been there at the time...when it was a' happenin'...know whit Ah mean?"

Archie shrugged.

"If you had've been there at the time, ye'd definitely be kickin' up the daisies noo," he grunted.

Charlie brought his hand up to his mouth and stifled a laugh.

"Come on," Archie said, "let's find oorsel's a pew for the night."

"A good idea!" Tom agreed. The men chose their beds near the front of the church and away from the doors.

"Hey!" Tom cried, "Under the seat...the pipes are still warm!"

"That'll be for the worshippers in the moarnin'!" Charlie said, adding, "kick yer shoes aff and get yer auld tootsies heated!"

The men discarded their tattered shoes and wallowed in the luxury of the central heating system...wriggling their toes and sighing at the sheer pleasure of it all. They each lay under a pew, one in front of the other, and glorified God and his plumbing.

"D'ye no' think we should have a few words wi' HIM...thankin' HIM for his hospitality?" Charlie whispered.

"Aye, Ah think we should," Archie agreed, "it's only right, so it is. Go on, Tom...you're the educated wan amongst us!"

Tom gave a slight cough to cover up his embarrassment, although he was delighted at the compliment.

"Aye, well...er..." he hesitated, "let's see, noo...er...Beggin' yer pardon, Lord, Ah hope ye will forgive us for burstin' intae yer hoose like this. We wull pay for the windae immediately we are cognizant of some money.

"Y'see, we've naewhere else tae go...and, as you wull no doubt know, it would freeze the...er...freeze ye oot there the night, so it would."

His prayer was interrupted by Charlie and Wullie's "Hear, Hear!"

Tom continued:

"We didnae like tae come in when the place was packed. Ah mean...well...who would want tae sit beside us, eh? Know whit Ah mean? And we're no' a' that good, y'see! It's been years since any o' us has graced yer hoose wi' oor presence. Ah widnae expect that you would have missed us, mind ye. But we feel a bit ashamed creepin' in like this...just because we happened tae be cauld. We'll no' take anythin'...we are not thieves, y'now! Sorry we had only tuppence for yer wee boax. If we had mair we would have gied ye mair. Although, tae be truthful if we had mair we might have been tempted for tae buy a fish supper between us. Anywey, we're sorry...and we like yer wee crib. We were just sayin' it would've been nice tae have been there...so, thanks again for the pew!"

Charlie and Archie slapped Tom on the back:

"Well done!" Charlie said, "Ah couldnae have done better masel'!"

"Me, tae!" Archie agreed.

"Aye, well...er...let's get doon for the night," Tom said, a little embarrassed, "we'll leave the caun'les till breakfast time."

The men settled down as best they could. They closed their eyes, cosily enveloped in the warmth and soon fell into deep and peaceful slumber.

Father Connolly opened up the huge doors at seven-thirty in the morning to get things prepared for the first mass at eight o'clock. Old Annie arrived at the same moment in the full knowledge that the good father was always punctual.

"A nice service last night, Father!" she complimented.

"Ah, thanks, Annie," Father Connolly said, awaiting Annie's

moans about the untidyness left by the good folk of the previous night. They walked down the centre aisle together. As expected, Annie would grunt a complaint now and again as she picked up discarded hymn books and leaflets. Annie suddenly let out a cry.

"Would ye look at this, Father!" she bellowed.

Father Connolly hurried to her side to see what caused the commotion.

"Look!" Annie cried, trying to contain herself, "would ye look at THAT!" she snapped, pointing down between the pews. "Three pairs of dirty, smelly shoes!" she wailed, pinching her nose. "WHO would kick their manky shoes aff and jist leave them there tae stink the place oot, eh?"

Father Connolly had rarely seen Annie so angry!

"Maybe somebody's feet were bothering them," he said innocently. "Just take them out and dump them, Annie."

"They look like they could walk oot themsel's," Annie grumbled, picking up the shoes and holding them at arms length. Annie threw the shoes into a corner and continued with her 'inspection'.

Arriving at the crib, she stopped and gazed at the Christmas scene before her and was joined by the good priest.

"Aye," he sighed, "it must've been lovely to have been there at that moment, Annie, eh?"

Annie nodded: "Aye, an' you're a fly wan, Father, so ye are!"

"What d'ye mean?" Father Connolly asked, furrowing his brows.

"Look at the crib!" Annie said, "Ah knew there was somethin' missin'...but you widnae accept that Ah was right..."

"Ach, what are ye talkin' about, Annie?" Father Connolly grunted.

"LOOK!" Annie cried, pointing to the crib and feeling pleased with herself. "Ye sneaked them in there when Ah wisnae lookin', didn't ye, eh?...Them there...THEY THREE WISE MEN...!"

Father Connolly rubbed his glasses with his hankie, bent down and looked closely into the crib. Annie was right! The Three Wise Men were there in their obligatory positions...at the feet of the baby.

"Did ye get them in a sale, Father?" Annie asked with a chuckle, "Ah mean, look...wan's got his big toe missin'."

They did not hear the cheery chortle echoing round the church...in triplicate!